THE HOLLYWOOD **BOOK TEN** 1956 MURDER MYSTERIES

A DEADLY SHOOT in TEXAS

PETER S. FISCHER

www.petersfischer.com

ALSO BY PETER S. FISCHER

Me and Murder, She Wrote
Expendable: A Tale of Love and War
The Blood of Tyrants
The Terror of Tyrants

The Hollywood Murder Mystery Series

Jezebel in Blue Satin
We Don't Need No Stinking Badges
Love Has Nothing to Do With It
Everybody Wants An Oscar
The Unkindness of Strangers
Nice Guys Finish Dead
Pray For Us Sinners
Has Anybody Here Seen Wyckham?
Eyewitness to Murder
A Deadly Shoot in Texas
Everybody Let's Rock
A Touch of Homicide
Some Like 'Em Dead
Dead Men Pay No Debts
The Death of Her Yet
Dead and Buried

A Deadly Shoot in Texas

Copyright © 2014

ISBN 978-1523350650

To my good friend, Jerry Orbach
.... you are sorely missed.

PROLOGUE

"It's going to be the number one box office hit of 1956," the man says.

"No," I say.

"It's going to win the Oscar for Best Picture."

"You've been saying that for years and you haven't been right since 1943."

"It's based on a prize winning novel by the eminent authoress Edna Ferber."

" So was 'So Big' and you know what happened to that movie."

"Rock Hudson."

"Nice guy. So what?"

"Elizabeth Taylor."

"My dream girl. Still not enough."

"James Dean."

I stop short. That's interesting. Then I shake my head. Not interesting enough. "I've met him. A nice young man but woefully miscast."

The man is starting to turn pink.

"God damn it, Bernardi, what do you want from me?"

"Freedom and I already have it."

Jack Warner leans forward on his desk and fixes me with a hard stare.

"You owe me," he says.

Uh-oh. I have no response for that one.

"Do you remember what you said to me two years ago when I let you leave this company?"

"You didn't let me leave, Jack. I quit."

"You couldn't quit. You had a contract."

"I never had a contract. Jack, you're getting senile in your old age."

"I gave you a nice severance package."

"It was generous," I say. "One for your side."

"And do you know what you said? Do you remember, Joe?"

"I remember."

"If you ever need me for something, Jack, I'll be there for you. You remember saying those words, Joe?"

"Yes, I remember."

"Well, there you are," Jack Warner says with a self-satisfied smile on his face. He sits back in his fancy padded leather chair and re-lights his smelly Havana cigar. He smiles. His teeth are white and sharp like a shark's.

I spent seven years of my life working for this man at one of the biggest and best studios in town and I'll be the first to admit, it wasn't all bad. For six of those seven years I was chief assistant to the Vice President of Press and Publicity, Charlie Berger. I learned a lot and met a lot of fabulous people and I might have stayed at Warner Brothers for the rest of my career except for one thing. In my seventh year Charlie Berger retired and I took over his job. This is akin to being an anonymous functionary in a sea of flunkies and then having to stand in front of Robin Hood's target when he is a scant six feet away and in a foul mood. Daily meetings, evening reports, weekend brainstorming and second guessing by the barrel. I finally gave up and went into a partnership with a feisty earth mother named Bertha Bowles and in two years we have become a major player in artist management and film publicity. So why am I here sitting across from this almost likeable cobra? Because I am a man of my word. Bertha has told me that my inate honesty in this business will someday destroy me. She may be right.

"I left you in good shape with Dexter Craven," I say.

"Craven was a moron," Jack says.

"Not when he was working for me," I say.

"Your standards are lower than mine," he says.

"What did you do to him?"

"Nothing. He slipped up on a press conference. I pointed out how neglectful he was—"

"In what tone of voice?"

"My usual."

"Oh, great," I mutter.

"He started to cry. I suggested crying was not the mark of a Warner Brothers employee."

"And what did he do?"

"He started crying harder. God damned little wimp," Jack growls. "I told him you wouldn't cry like that. Be like Joe, I told him. Have some balls."

"Well, that was one way to deal with him. I take it he quit."

"Hell, no, I fired his bony ass. I never would have fired you, Joe. You were the best. Still are."

"Is all this flattery designed to get me to say yes?" I say.

"All I want is a simple yes or no. Will you take on 'Giant' for me?"

"You understand, Jack, that if I say yes, you are retaining Bowles & Bernardi, not just me."

"Of course."

"On our regular fee schedule."

"Which is?"

I tell him. He almost chokes on the remaining stub of the cigar.

"Can I assume that means you're not interested? Excellent, Jack. Nice talking to you after all this time." I stand up and reach across the desk, my hand extended in comradeship. He glares up at me.

"You're hired," he growls.

I return to my office a whipped dog. I could never get the better of the man. I still can't. On the other hand if I am going to get involved with another Warner Brothers film, I could do a lot worse than 'Giant'. George Stevens directing and stars galore. All of that might be just enough to counteract the curse of J.L. Warner.

"What did he say when you turned him down?" Bertha wants to know. Bertha's the pragmatist in this partnership. I am sometimes given to sentimental flights of fancy. Not Bertha. She's grounded like a fifty-foot lightning rod. Now she is smiling at me, waiting for my answer. When she doesn't get it her eyes narrow into wary little slits.

"You DID turn him down, Joe?"

"Not in so many words," I say.

"You only needed one word, Joe. No. That is one word. That is THE one word." She throws up her hands. "I've been angling for a week to get Otto Preminger's new picture. 'Land of the Pharaohs' is dying out there and needs a shot of adrenalin and this kid Robert Francis from 'The Caine Mutiny' is looking for a manager and some decent press. And what does my partner do? He indentures himself to Hollywood's Mr. Warmth for a picture that will not be released for at least a year. Mark my words, Joe. George Stevens in an editing room is not a love affair, it is a long term marriage. He will be cutting this picture until late next year and maybe, just maybe, he'll have it ready for the following year's Oscars. And all the while you will be sitting around pulling your pud while actual business floats away because you haven't time to handle it, because Boy Scout that you are, you made some dumb promise years ago to Jack Warner."

"I quoted him a fee for services, Bertha," I tell her.

"Oh, yes, I can't wait to hear the kind of money we're going to be making from Old Bargain Basement."

I give her the quote. She stares at me not quite sure she heard correctly.

"Come again?" she says.

Obligingly I come again.

"That's more money than we have ever gotten from anybody for any project at any time," Bertha says quietly.

"I know. I took our highest fee to date, doubled it in anticipation of the usual interference and aggravation and added another ten percent just for the hell of it."

"And he agreed?"

"Not only that, he gave me a good faith retainer." I reach in my pocket and take out a check which I hand to her. She looks at it, then holds it closer and squinting, looks at it again.

"Is that first number a 3 or an 8?" she asks.

"It's an 8, Bertha," I say.

She smiles at me.

"Give me a few moments to book your reservation to Texas."

CHAPTER ONE

I'm sitting at the bar in this dingy little cantina in a nowhere town in the middle of one of America's biggest sand piles. For starters I am looking for a little peace and quiet. I arrived in Marfa, Texas, three mornings ago by train from Los Angeles and immediately found myself in the middle of a Ringling Brothers extravaganza. I am sure that prior to a month ago this tiny dot on the Lone Star map was a peaceful, almost sleepy little town with very little overt excitement to rattle the natives out of their humdrum lives. No more. A movie company has taken over and things may never be the same. The Hotel Paisano has been bought out by Warner Brothers to house its film crew. Star struck residents have turned their houses over to the picture's principal players and anyone who can walk and talk is vying to become an extra in one of the film's many crowd scenes. If there is any other topic of conversation going around I have yet to hear it. A dozen reporters from America's biggest newspapers are on hand, scattered in private homes in every corner of the town. The local movie theater, The Palace, has already started showing the various stars' biggest motion pictures. Tonight they're featuring 'East of Eden'. I was caught chatting this afternoon with Carroll Baker and afterwards a dozen locals asked me for my autograph. I was chased into the hotel and one matronly lady actually followed me to my room, convinced that I was Richard Conte and wouldn't take no for an answer. She left only after I signed Conte's name in her autograph book.

The noise of the madding crowd is not my only problem. I am also trying to get drunk but I am not succeeding. This is depressing. I am not a problem drinker. Most often I drink beer in moderation but once in a while I tie one on with hard liquor and it almost always occurs in response to some major frustration in my life over which I have no power. I got plastered when I realized that Bunny, my beautiful live-in and the lady of my life, had walked out on me. It also happened when I was told that the second lady in my life had deliberately gotten herself pregnant with my child without so much as a polite 'May I please?' And now here I am in this wretched little dump on the outskirts of Marfa throwing back Jim Beam like it was soda pop and I'm just as sober as I was forty-five minutes ago when I walked into the place.

There's a name for west Texas in July and it is never uttered in polite company. The temperature often climbs above 100, the dust threatens to choke the life out of anything that moves, and the wind cuts and slashes at whatever stands in its way. Our two leading men, Rock Hudson and James Dean, pretend to be unaffected by conditions but they are playing their own private game of 'chicken'. Neither will be the first to complain. I am waiting for one of them to emerge from his air conditioned trailer to sun himself buck naked while lying on a sand dune. Macho has taken on a whole new meaning. Meanwhile Liz Taylor endures, always looking fresh, never a drop of sweat to mar her patrician beauty. Scorpions, rattlers and gila monsters thrive while the movie company suffers, not always in silence.

I glance at my watch. It reads twenty minutes past midnight. Until a few minutes ago I was alone here except for Pepe the bartender.

Pepe is a rotund fellow with a happy disposition who reminds me a lot of Thomas Gomez. He is half-owner of this down at the heels establishment of which he is very proud. Fifteen years ago he was a busboy at a local restaurant and his English was limited to things like 'Good morning' and 'Thank you'. I doubt he is here legally though I suspect nobody really cares. He is married with two little girls and perhaps another on the way. Secretly he hopes for a son but is resigned to the fact that God will decide.

I look up from my glass and realize that we've been joined by an attractive young lady at the far end of the bar who seems to be nursing a 7 and 7. There have been times in my life when I would have gotten up, slid smoothly onto the stool next to her and made scintillating small talk until I had her firmly under the covers in some nearby bedroom. Not tonight and not her. Close examination leads me to believe that she is barely 20 years old, if that. And besides, my thoughts, painful though they may be, are all about Bunny. Until six weeks ago she was calling me faithfully at the end of the month sounding as chipper and adoring as always. And then on June 30, no call. I leave for Texas on July 9. Still no call and now there is no way for her to reach me unless she phones my secretary, Glenda Mae, to learn where I am. It is now Tuesday, July 12. No call. No letter. No contact. I am depressed beyond reason. As far as I'm concerned the whole human race can go to hell.

I finish my drink and rap on the bar with my empty glass. Pepe nods and approaches with my pal, Jim Beam, and pours a refill. I believe this is number six. Pepe is astounded that I haven't fallen to the floor. I tell him I wouldn't give the floor the satisfaction. At that moment I become aware that I have company. I look to my right. There on the adjoining stool is the cute young babe from across the way, an unlit cigarette between the fingers of her right hand and her drink in her left.

"Got a light?" she asks, just like Lauren Bacall in 'To Have and

Have Not'. I'm fascinated by this question because there are at least a half-dozen ashtrays on the bar and each one of them has a fresh book of matches attached.

"Sure," I say, taking the book from the ashtray directly in front of me. I light her cigarette and she inhales deeply before letting the smoke drift out of her nose. Now that I see her close up, I am even more impressed. Her skin has a slight olive tint and her lustrous black hair bespeaks at least a partial Hispanic heritage. Her eyes are gorgeous and permanently flirtatious. I will struggle against doing something stupid but it will be difficult.

"Thanks," she says. "I'm Stella."

"Joe."

"Nice to meet you, Joe. Waiting for somebody?"

"Nope."

"I was supposed to meet a fella here at midnight."

She makes a production of slowly letting her gaze swivel across the room. "Guess he got lost." She drains the rest of her drink and sets the glass on the bar, then looks at me expectantly. What the hell, I'm on an expense account. I can afford to buy the girl a drink. I signal to Pepe and point to her glass. He nods and starts to fix her a fresh one.

"You live around here?" she asks.

"I'm in town on business," I say. "How about you? Here for the movie?"

"Visiting a friend. A classmate."

"Where do you go to school?" I ask.

"UT in Austin. I start my final year in six weeks."

"I like your football team."

"I don't. You want to go somewhere?"

Wow, I think. These young kids. No semblance of subtlety. Pepe places her fresh drink in front of her.

"Go where?" I ask as if I didn't know.

"You know," she says. "Go somewhere."

"I'm pretty sure most of the local saloons are closed by now."

"I'm not talking about saloons. I'm pissed and lonely and you'll do."

"In that case I don't think so," I say.

"I'm not a whore if that's what you're thinking."

"Never entered my mind."

She frowns. The little nymphet isn't used to rejection.

"Is there something wrong with me?" she asks.

"Yeah. Your birth certificate."

"I know what I'm doing," she says.

"I'll bet you do," I reply.

"Relax, mister. You can't get me in trouble. Not now. I guarantee it," she says bitterly.

At that moment the phone rings. Pepe walks over and answers it. After a few seconds he looks in our direction.

"You Stella?" he asks.

"That's me." she says, getting off the stool and moving to the other end of the bar where she takes the phone from Pepe. She turns her back on me and I can't hear a word she says. After a minute or so, she hangs up. She comes back and grabs her purse.

"Nice meeting you," she says as she heads for the door.

"Same here," I say as she goes outside.

I turn my attention back to my drink. A missed opportunity? I don't think so. I'm 36 years old, not quite dead yet, but I draw the line at college kids, even if they're legal. A man should have some semblance of propriety. I take another sip of my drink and decide it's time to start considering if I should think about going back to the hotel for a good night's sleep. Yes, this will definitely require some thought and I'm going to do that very shortly. Maybe one more drink just to stimulate my thought processes. Pepe is reading my mind because he approaches with Jim Beam in hand. As he pours he directs my attention to a sign above the cash register. "We Close at One. No Exceptions." I nod in understanding.

I look out the front window. Stella is right outside, pacing expectantly. At that moment a white Corvette convertible pulls up. The guy behind the wheel looks young and he's blonde but that's all I can make out for sure. Stella hops in the car and it pulls away into the night. I check my watch again. Twenty minutes to one. Enough is enough, I think. I get up, asking Pepe what I owe. He tells me and I lay a twenty on the bar. Pepe's happy. I'm not because I'm still sober.

I leave the bar and start walking north on Highland Street toward the Hotel Paisano where I have a very small room. Marfa is far from a big town. The population is only 3600 even though it's the county seat. Like I said, west Texas is a great place to live if you're a tarantula. It's twelve blocks to the hotel and I make it in twenty minutes. I enter the lobby which is deserted except for one elderly lady sitting in an easy chair, fast asleep, an open book in her lap. No one from the company is up and about. The morning call for crew is six o'clock and George Stevens, who has been directing for twenty six years with time out for a distinguished stint in the Army during WWII, doesn't tolerate slackers or sleep deprived zombies. He's a taskmaster but he knows what he's doing and he gets the job done. No one in his right mind crosses him.

I go to my room. I check for messages and finding none, I get ready for a decent night's sleep. I needn't set the alarm. Six o'clock for crew. Eight o'clock for the performers. As for me, I set my own schedule. Most likely I will wander over to transportation around ten for a ride out to the set. No one will notice and those that do won't care. For the time being I'm getting acquainted, buttering up the visiting press and looking for the right approach to publicizing the picture. James Dean is a natural centerpiece. After 'Rebel Without a Cause' and 'East of Eden' he's become a teen icon. I start there. Where I go next is anyone's guess.

In the meantime, I endure. The weather report for tomorrow is for more of the same. Heat, wind and a town full of gawkers who couldn't tell Roddy McDowell from Sydney Greenstreet. I'm atingle with anticipation.

CHAPTER TWO

he next morning I'm up with the scorpions. The real ones. Not the out-of-town reporters. I want to get a jump on things at the location in the flatlands west of town and if the crew can get up at 5:30, then by God so can I. I decide to make one quick check of things at the production office on the lower level. Big mistake. A couple of go-getters are busy setting up shop but there is nothing urgent for me on the message board. I look over at a table where we keep copies of the most recent outgoing press releases. An old woman is leafing through them curiously. I don't recognize her and something tells me she's a fan who is not minding her own business.

"Excuse me," I say. "Can I help you?"

"You sure can, Joe. Feel free to start anytime you like," she says looking up at me. I still don't recognize the face but I couldn't miss that voice in an unlit coal mine.

"Sorry, Miss McCambridge," I say. "I didn't recognize you."

"Most people don't before I've put my face on."

I mentioned 'old' but in reality Mercedes McCambridge is only 40. She's right about one thing. She doesn't wear well without the war paint. Seven years ago she won an Oscar and she'd been around a while before that.

"Can I help you look for something?" I ask.

"I'm checking to see if you have another release from that fat fool from the Sun-Times. My hometown paper, I'm sorry to say. Three days ago he wrote me up like I was a has-been back from the dead, overweight and uncooperative. Also the picture he sent along would have looked good on my driver's license."

"I'm afraid we don't have much control about what these reporters write. I'll take the rap for the photo but he's a local. My own photographer is coming in this afternoon and believe me Willie is the best. We'll make it up to you."

"Well, I sure hope so, Joe. I've had one lousy picture in the past five years, a stinker of a western with Joan Crawford and I want to make the most of this picture and this part."

"Count on me," I say.

"Really? Well, I'd sure like to believe that, Joe, but from what the press boys have been saying, you're phoning this one in."

I look at her sharply. I know I've had a lot on my mind and it's true, there are a lot of press people in town, each needing to be babied and catered to, but I was pretty sure I was on top of things. Now I may have to reexamine that.

"Not true, Miss McCambridge. We'll meet later today and we'll bat something out you'll be happy with. Promise."

She looks up at me with a grin.

"Hey, if you can't believe a press agent, who can you believe?"

I can't help myself. I laugh.

It takes twenty minutes to get out to the location and once there I make a beeline for the craft services tent. Craft services is like a free snack shop for cast and crew to nosh at during the day and is operated by the caterer. I have missed breakfast and I intend to rectify that oversight immediately.

"You don't remember me, do you?"

I look to my left. There is Rock Hudson, buttering a croissant as he smiles down at me and even though I am six-one, believe me, he smiles down on me as I'm cracking open a hard boiled egg.

"Sure I do, Roy," I smile back, "but I wasn't going to mention it until you did."

I call him Roy because that's how he introduced himself to me five years ago when I met him in a homosexual bar in Los Angeles. Roy Fitzgerald, he said to me. It was his birth name. Although he was under contract to Universal Studios, he was not yet widely known as Rock Hudson.

"The how and the where of our meeting is not something I talk about," Rock says.

"In that case I won't talk about it either," I tell him.

"Thanks. So that guy we were trying to rescue from the heavy hitters, whatever happened to him?"

"They caught up with him. Fatally."

"Too bad," Rock says. "He seemed like a nice man."

"Nice but weak and in over his head."

Hubbell Cox, an obvious homosexual, made the mistake of crossing the wrong person. Rock and I helped him escape from the bar but his safety was short lived. By the end of the day he and his male lover were shot to death in a beach house in Malibu.

"Sorry to hear it," Rock says and I know he means it. I don't know Rock well but the little I know and everything I've heard pegs the man as one of the decent people in our business. "How long are you going to be with us?" he asks me.

"I'm not sure. I have a photographer coming in this afternoon who will grab a boatload of stills of everybody and everything."

"We have somebody we've been using," Rock says.

"A local. I've seen his work. It's okay, but we can do a lot better."

"You're the boss,'" he says taking a huge bite of the croissant.

"Yeah, that's one of the ways I kid myself," I say. "Hey, while I've got you, I had heard months ago that Grace Kelly had been signed for the part of Leslie. What happened?"

Rock shakes his head.

"And Bill Holden was supposed to play my part. When that fell through, they made me an offer which I jumped at. George also gave me my choice of leading ladies, Grace or Elizabeth. Elizabeth is a legend and Grace has been making noises like she's going to marry that prince over in Europe so it wasn't a hard decision. You know Elizabeth, don't you, Joe?"

"We've met a couple of times but I wouldn't say I know her."

"You're going to love her. Brimming with talent and she's got a heart of gold." He checks his watch. "Uh-oh. I think I'm due in makeup. See you on the set."

He walks off as I sprinkle salt and pepper on my egg. Along with a container of coffee, this is what passes for breakfast. I would have eaten at the hotel but the dining room was full of tourists with a forty minute wait. The Old Borunda Cafe wasn't much better. I start to worry that this town is going to turn me into a grouchy old man.

"That's not much of a breakfast," she says.

I turn around and Flavia Hernandez is smiling at me. She's 19, cute as a kitten and the daughter of Pedro and Maria who run the craft services operation. From what I can tell every guy on the crew has his eye on her. When she's on duty, they come from far and wide for an apple, a soda or a kind word. They can get all three but that's as far as it goes. Mom and Pop keep a close eye on her and besides, yesterday she told me she has her heart set on medical school. She's going into her sophomore year at the University of Texas in Austin and free time is for studying. According to her parents, she has no time for boys

"Let me fix you an omelet," she says.

"Thanks, but this is fine," I tell her.

"You're too skinny."

"I call it slim and sinewy," I tell her.

"Call it whatever you like, Mr. B. I think you could use an omelet."

"Tomorrow, Flavia. Promise."

She smiles. "I'll hold you to it."

"By the way, I meant to ask you, when do you go back to school?"

"Third week in August," she says. "I should be here for most of the filming."

"Good," I say, "I'd miss your smiling face."

With a wave, I walk off. I think this may be a good time to re-introduce myself to Elizabeth who is here without husband Michael Wilding. Wilding is off somewhere in Asia filming a movie about an Afghan rebel named Zadak. From what I hear it's a paycheck and not much more.

I exit the tent and am hit full on by the glare of the morning sun. The heat comes along with it and almost immediately I can feel moisture bursting forth in my armpits. I start toward the trailer encampment which is about fifty yards away. Here I will find wardrobe, hair and makeup, camera equipment, props, and the individual trailers for our stars and the director. As I approach the closest trailer I spot James Dean, shirtless and wearing cutoff Levis hovering over the open trunk of a sleek white sports car. There's a wrench in his hand and a tool box at his feet. He looks as if he knows what he's doing.

"Good morning," I say.

He looks up and I think he's smiling. It's hard to say because he's squinting into the sun.

"Hi," he says.

As I get close I see it's not the trunk at all he's working on but the engine compartment which is at the rear of the car, not the front.

"Interesting," I say. "Just like a Volkswagen."

He looks up at me with a look of annoyance.

"Oh, no, man, this little bastard is nothing like a Volkswagen."

"Little bastard?"

Dean laughs quietly.

"Yeah, that's what Jack Warner called me when he found out I was racing cars so now I call my cars little bastards in honor of the big bastard. Now this car here is a Porsche. That's German."

"Sorry. I'm not much on sports cars," I tell him.

"It's called a Super Speedster. Goes like a bat out of hell, but you gotta treat it right. I finished first in it at the Bakersfield races on May 1st."

"You know, I had no idea you raced."

"Oh, yeah. Just started a few months ago. I'm gonna get real good at it as soon as Warner gets out of my face. The son of a bitch got it put in my contract. No racing while I'm working on one of his pictures. I gotta find me a new studio."

I grin. "Can I quote you on that?"

He looks at me puzzled, then giggles knowingly.

"Wait a minute. I know you. You're the publicity guy."

I extend my hand. "Joe Bernardi. We met on the set of 'East of Eden'. Kazan introduced us."

"Sure, I remember. Sorry, my hand's all greasy, Joe, but it's nice to see you again." In those days, Dean was the special project of my boss, Charlie Berger. On orders from Warner, no one else in publicity went near him. Charlie's chief job was to convince the press and America's teeny girls that Dean was an eligible bachelor when he was anything but. Although he'd been enamored of Pier Angeli and had a fling with Ursula Andress, he'd also had too many liaisons with gentlemen friends to be called available, let alone eligible. This is not just my personal opinion or the product of gossip. When Dean registered for the draft, he identified himself as a homosexual.

"Any problem with me publicizing your racing activities, Mr. Dean?"

"Hell, no. I'd love it, and Jesus, man, the name's Jim," Dean says sheepishly.

"Good human interest," I say. "Any races on the horizon?"

"October first, Salinas, California. George says we'll be wrapped by then."

"My photographer's coming in this afternoon, Jim. We'll get a barrel full of photos and then you and I will set aside maybe an hour or two on one of your off days to chat."

He snorts. "Off days. That's funny. Damned few of those around," he says and then he smiles. "We'll work it out, Joe. Looking forward to it."

We chat for a few more minutes and I learn that Elizabeth won't be arriving on the set until late afternoon. Stevens and I have already had a long conversation about publicity. He's the producer as well as the director so when it comes to plans of action, he has several votes. Lucky for me, a few of his close friends who know my work have told him to leave me alone and he says he will. Also lucky for me, he didn't ask what I had in mind. When I figure it out I'll let him know.

I wander up toward the Reata ranch house which really isn't a house at all but an empty facade. The interior scenes will be filmed back in Burbank on a sound stage. For a non-house it's an imposing structure, three stories high and standing tall in the middle of nowhere. At the moment, Stevens is directing a scene with Chill Wills and Jane Withers near the front door. A couple of hundred yards away, behind restraining ropes, a sea of onlookers is taking it all in. In the spirit of amity, Stevens has declared open sets for all exterior shooting which means the townfolk and the tourists are welcome to come watch the filming and now and then, when possible, mix with the stars between set-ups.

I look around for my driver. His name is Skeeter Todd and besides being a very nice young man, he's the quarterback for the Marfa High School football team. I catch his eye and he waves in understanding. A minute later he pulls up in a battered old station wagon which he owns and we head back toward town. When it comes to transportation, the stars get brand new town cars and limos, the rest of us get pot luck. Like everything else in short supply, transportation is at the top of the list. The local car rental firms have been cleaned out and the cabs are so busy they hardly have time to fill up with gas. Skeeter's no different than most Marfa natives. He's star struck and has shaken the hand of Rock Hudson. When he learns that I actually know Marlon Brando the questions come fast and furious and when I assure him that Brando is a very bright and pleasant man, I make his day.

We're tooling along eastbound on Rte. 90 heading for the center of town when we come up to S. Tenison Street where three county squad cars are parked across the way. About fifty yards into the brush several uniformed cops are hovering over something that I can't see. Skeeter slows down to rubberneck just as an ambulance comes wailing up to the intersection. Two white-clad men hop out and hurriedly carry a stretcher out to the cops.

"What do you think, Mr. B?" Skeeter asks, still straining for a good look.

"Nothing good, Skeeter," I say, "but I think we'd better keep out of their way and you'd better keep your eye on the road."

"Sure as shootin'," he says, one of his favorite expressions. Reluctantly he returns his attention to his driving and ten minutes later we pull up in front of the hotel. He asks if I'm going to need him again today and I tell him I doubt it. Most everything I'm ever going to need in Marfa is within walking distance and I won't be visiting the set again today. He grins and drives off. His girlfriend's name is Cheryl Ann and she hustles banana splits at the local ice cream parlor. In an emergency I know where to find him.

As soon as I enter the lobby of the hotel, I hear her voice.

"About time you showed up. I was ready to send out the dogs."

I turn and there's Willie, hand on hip, regarding me with

undisguised annoyance. Wearing her usual Army surplus jacket, faded dungarees and cruddy unpolished combat boots, Wilhelmina May Popkin is a vision of unkempt disarray. Her makeup, what little she uses, is mussed and her hair looks like it's been rearranged by an egg beater. The three cameras hanging around her neck reveal her for what she is, a wannabe Margaret Bourke-White covering insurrections in every part of the globe. Instead she is here with me in Marfa taking publicity stills for a movie because we pay a lot better than some third tier news magazine that has trouble meeting a monthly payroll.

I walk over to her and give her a big hug and whisper in her ear. "You need a bath," I say.

"Damned right I do but I'm not going to get one here. They got no room for me, boss."

"Yes, they do. It's taken care of," I say.

She head nods toward the desk where an officious looking young man with less hair than a light bulb is poring over some papers. "Well, tell it to Sammy Skinhead over there. He knows from nothin'."

I go to the desk and approach Sammy whose name is actually Lance according to his name tag. He is irritatingly self-important when he tells me there is no room at the inn for my trusted co-worker. She is not registered. She was never registered. In his eyes she is a non-person. I grab Willie by the elbow and steer her toward the staircase. Downstairs we make our way to the production office which is alive with activity. I spot the unit manager, Tom Andre, off in a corner gently berating one of the locals for some minor transgression. Tom runs a tight ship. He does not tolerate shoddy or careless work. The local moves out, head bowed, and I move in.

"Tom," I say. "Say hello to Willie Popkin."

Tom, who is in a dour mood, manages to eke out a grudging hello.

"So Tom, where's her room?"

"What room?"

"Two days ago I told you she was coming. I told you to get her a room."

"Oh," he says, frowning.

"What do you mean, oh?"

Tom sighs. "We have a big shortage of rooms."

"I know that."

"When you said get Willie a room, I put her in with Floyd Crabtree, the hairdresser."

"What!" I say in disbelief.

"You told me Willie! God damn it, Bernardi, I'm not a friggin' mindreader."

"Fine," I growl. "Move Floyd."

"I can't. He comes with Elizabeth Taylor."

"Just great," I grouse. "Get Willie a room."

"Did you not hear me? There are no rooms!" Tom shouts.

We're nose to nose. Fisticuffs are next.

"Hold it, fellas!" Willie says coming between us. She turns to Tom. "This Floyd. Would you say he's a little—" She breaks off and waves a limp wrist in front of Tom's nose.

"No, I'd say he's a lot," Tom growls impatiently

She shrugs.

"Fine. No problem. Just make sure there are two beds."

I look at Willie. "You don't have to do this."

"Hey, boss, I said no problem." She looks over at Tom. "However, if you're lying to me about Floyd's libido, he's going to be singing soprano at the wrap party. You get my drift?"

"I get it," Tom says.

I tell Tom to get Willie moved into the room. I tell Willie to take a bath and make herself look presentable and I'll meet her in the hotel bar in an hour. I head for my room.

I sigh. My room. It isn't much. It may even be less than that. It has a narrow twin sized bed, a wobbly night table with lamp and phone, a skinny dresser with three drawers, and a Salvation Army table upon which sits a totally unreliable 10" television set. Just to the left of it is a narrow door that opens onto a postage-sized balcony that overlooks the rear of the restaurant next door, principally the area where the garbage is stacked for pickup. Meanwhile back in the room, the closet is even skimpier than the balcony and comes with four hangers. I use them all to hang up my two suits and two sports outfits and I'm out of space. The bathroom has a sink, a commode and a bathtub that would cramp up Mickey Rooney. Oh, yes, and they have supplied me with a towel, a bar of soap, and one roll of toilet paper.

I flip on the TV to the local news broadcast, strip down and go into the bathroom for a quick bath. As the tub is filling with hot water I sneak a glance at myself in the full length mirror on the back of the bathroom door. Slim and sinewy, no question about it. Flavia is all wrong.

When I emerge from the bathroom, toweling off, I spot the little blinking red light on my phone. I thought I'd heard it ring but wasn't sure. I check and as I suspected Jack Warner is trying to get a hold of me. Well, I can't duck him forever so I return the call.

"What's going on down there, Joe?" Warner growls. The man growls a lot except when he wants something from you in which case he purrs.

"Same old same old, Jack," I say, "though it looks like we have a happy set despite the crappy weather conditions."

"Have you seen the dailies?"

"Some. They look pretty good though Stevens seems to be shooting a lot of film."

"A lot. Yeah, I'd say a lot. The son of a bitch probably owns stock in Eastman the way he's burning negative."

"It's the way he shoots, Jack. You knew that when you hired him."

"I didn't hire him. He came with the picture, God damn it."

Jack mumbles and grumbles for another minute or two and I listen. Something else is bothering him. I can always tell.

"What else, Jack? Stevens isn't your only complaint."

"No, it's Disney."

"What about him?"

"This Sunday he's opening that damned amusement park down in Anaheim and suckered me into saying I'd be there."

"Well, what's the problem, J.L.?"

"Come on, Joe. We're in the movie business, not the Coney Island business. It's bad enough I'm getting into television, the next thing you know we'll all be opening up hootchy-kootchy parlors in downtown Daytona."

He rants on like this for several more minutes before he has to hang up and take a call from his brother Harry in New York. His parting instructions to me are to tell George Stevens to stop using so much film. I tell him I will though I have no intention of doing so. Stevens is Jack's problem, not mine.

Now I glance over at the TV news show which is reporting a grisly murder just discovered a few miles out of town. Right away I know it's the scene Skeeter and I witnessed on our way back to the hotel. Details are sketchy. The victim is a young woman, identity unknown. The preliminary finding is death by strangulation. If there was more to learn, I don't get it because just then there is a knock at my door. I answer it. Standing there, half-leaning on her duffle bag, is Willie.

"Floyd already has a new roommate. His name is Lester and he's prettier than I am so like it or not, boss, you're stuck with me."

She hefts the duffle onto her shoulder and pushes her way past me. "Where's the rest of this room?" she asks looking around in disgust.

"Hold it, Willie," I say. "You can't stay here."

She shrugs.

"It's here or tomorrow morning I'm on the cannonball express back to L.A."

Eight minutes later Willie and I are back in the production office and I am once again jawing at Tom Andre who needs me like he needs hepatitis. There are no rooms. Not at this hotel. Not anywhere. Some of the locals grudgingly opened their houses to cast members but crew people are on their own. His voice is hovering several decibels above foghorn and everyone in the place is staring at us and I suddenly feel very small and mean-spirited. I put up my hands in surrender and take Willie by the arm. We retrace our steps toward the entrance.

At that moment, two Sheriff's deputies walk in and look around. The huskier one grabs me by the arm. He's got me by an inch and his muscles are bulging out of his tailored uniform. The name tag over his right hand pocket reads "Boggs".

"Which one is Tom Andre?" he asks.

I point. "That's him. The pink faced guy with the blood pressure problem."

Without a thank you, Boggs pushes past me and he and his partner make a beeline for Andre. My curiosity piqued, I'd like to go back and find out what this is all about but I have more pressing matters to attend to. I turn and look at Willie.

She smiles.

"I'm gonna need a bed," she says.

CHAPTER THREE

Usually I am awakened by sunlight streaming through my bedroom window. This morning it is pitch dark, my watch reads 5:52, and the room is filled with a noise I can only describe as a hippopotamus in the throes of an asthma attack. It sit bolt upright and as my eyes adjust to the darkness I can make out the rollaway bed over in the corner and the dark figure scrunched in a fetal position atop it's mattress. In that instant I make up my mind. Willie Popkin has got to go. If I can't find her a room elsewhere by the end of the day I am putting her on a train back to L.A. If there is no train, I will take her to the Greyhound station. If the busses aren't running, I'll stash her in the hallway with a pillow and a blanket.

Silently I creep out of my bed and into the bathroom. I brush my teeth and slip into yesterday's wardrobe, even down to my socks. Quietly I scoop up my wallet and watch and room key and edge out of the room, opening and closing the door with the greatest of care. I pray the dining room opens at six. It does. In fact it opened at five to accommodate the crew which has a 7:00 call out by the Reata ranch house. Bill Mellor, the director of photography and his camera operator are just finishing up and with their blessing I grab the empty seat at their table. I apologize for interrupting their conversation but Bill waves me off. Like everyone else this morning, they have been talking about the murder. It lead off the morning news show on the local channel and dominated the front page of the Big Bend Sentinel. So far, the facts are these. She was found in the scrub land off of Rte. 90, fully clothed but with no identification. Apparently she had been strangled but the official autopsy report is yet to come. The cops checked last evening with the unit manager, showing him a police photo of the victim, but as far as Andre could tell it wasn't anyone connected with the movie company. Apparently she was also not a local resident. Mellor shakes his head. Some murder, he snorts. Unknown victim, no witnesses, no evidence and no clues. Good luck with that. He checks his watch. Time to go, I tell him I'll see him out on the set.

The room thins out and I'm able to grab a waitress' attention. I wolf down two eggs over easy and a couple of sausage patties and drain them with a hot cup of joe before I amble over to the production office to check the shooting schedule which I forgot to pick up the night before. Today's going to be a big day and I see now why the crew got the early call. They're filming the barbecue scene which depicts the neighbors welcoming the newly married Leslie to the community. It's a big production scene with 60 to 70 extras and all the principals. The shoot will probably spill over to tomorrow and knowing what a meticulous director Stevens can be, perhaps even Saturday as well. Like Jack said, he's burning through film the way Sherman burned his way to the sea. The raw negative he's already used would add up to a dozen 'Gone With the Winds'.

I leave a message for Willie and then call Skeeter and tell him to meet me outside in fifteen minutes. Tom Andre is not around but one of his assistants tells me that the sheriff's deputies were here at least a half-hour last night before they finally left, no wiser than when they walked in.

As I head out the door I spot a copy of the morning paper on one of the tables and I grab it to read in the car on the way to the set. As expected Skeeter is waiting, motor running as I emerge from the hotel. I hop into the front seat and we take off. We're turning onto Rte 90 westbound when I finally unfold the paper to read a full account of the tragic death of that woman.

The first thing that hits me is the two column photo of the dead girl's face over the caption, "Do You Know This Woman?"

"Sweet Jesus," I mutter quietly.

"What's the matter?" Skeeter asks, taking his eyes off the road. The kid has a death wish. Now I know why his car is such a battered piece of junk.

"The dead girl. I know her," I say. "Two nights ago I was drinking with her in this two bit cantina at the edge of town."

"God's truth?" Skeeter asks, totally in awe.

"Absolutely. Try not to get us killed, Skeeter, while I read this."

I pore over the article carefully. The reporter, whose byline reads Nick Comstock, knows how to write a story but he's giving me a lot of color and not much information, mainly, I think, because the cops may not have had much to give him. They may also have a couple of hold-backs up their sleeve. A hold-back is a critical piece of information only the police know about so they can deal with the inevitable parade of whackos who will be showing up to confess to the killing.

And then my gaze falls on the seventh paragraph and I shake my head. No, this he's got wrong. Either that or the cops are all screwed up. In either case I can't keep what I know to myself.

"Skeeter, turn around. We're going back to town."

"Something wrong, Mr. B.?"

"You could say that."

The Presidio County Sheriff's headquarters is located on East Galveston Street just past Highland near the center of town. Three white cruisers with pale green trim and an ambulance are parked at the side of the building. A dozen cars half fill the visitors' parking lot. Skeeter makes thirteen. I get out of the car and head up the steps while Skeeter flips on a country-western radio station. The lettering on the glass door tells me the sheriff's name is Samuel Claxton. When I get inside I hand the desk sergeant my business card and ask to see Claxton. I'm told he is very busy but when I say I have information about the dead woman, the sergeant's attitude segues from disinterest to curiosity. I'm told to take a seat on a nearby bench. Someone will be with me shortly.

Sure enough, ten minutes later I'm being escorted to the back of the building and into the office of the man himself. Sam Claxton barely looks up as he gestures to a chair facing his desk. Whatever papers he's poring through on his desk, they have his full attention. After a few moments he slides the papers into a manila folder and then spins his chair around and rolls to a nearby filing cabinet. He files away the folder and closes the drawer and then rolls back to his desk. Even though he's sitting I can tell he's a tall man who takes care of himself. His complexion is ruddy and freckled and his sandy hair is close cropped, not quite a military crew cut. I put his age at about fifty. His eyes are a greenish brown and bore into mine, daring me to waste his time. He reaches over and picks up my business card from his desk and carefully checks it out.

"Well, Mr. Bernardi, I'm gonna assume from your dress and your demeanor that you are not some whack job here to confess to the killing," he says.

I assure him I am totally innocent and perfectly sane.

"The woman's name was Stella," I say.

"That so? Stella what?"

"I don't know. We met in a bar the evening before she was killed. We never got around to last names."

"Hooker?"

"No. College student. Said she was going back to Austin for her senior year at Texas."

"You tried to pick her up, that right?"

"Other way around," I say. "She was supposed to meet some guy. When it looked as if he'd stood her up, she got pissed like women sometimes do when their vanity is attacked."

"And you weren't interested," Claxton says.

"I'm not keen on twenty year olds, Sheriff."

"There's some that are, Mr. Bernardi. Even younger."

"I'm sure there are," I say. "I'm afraid, Sheriff, that you may have a bigger problem than just the young lady's identity."

"And what's that?"

"Stella walked into the bar about twenty after midnight. She left at ten minutes to one."

Claxton frowns.

"That's not possible."

"Maybe not but there it is. Your coroner puts the time of death between 8 and 9 p.m. Somewhere in writing his report, his pencil slipped. And don't take just my word for it. Pepe, the bartender, will back me up."

Claxton regards me curiously.

"I've known Doc Yardley all my life, Mr. Bernardi. He doesn't make mistakes, not ones like that. You have to be thinkin' of another girl."

"I don't think so." I reply.

"It's been my experience that when John Barleycorn is involved, the eyes and the brain don't always work together. Were you sober?"

"I believe I was."

"How many drinks had you had?" Claxton asks.

"Besides the point," I say.

"I don't think so. How many?" The folksiness has gone out of his voice replaced by something sharp and insistent.

"Five or six," I fudge.

He nods with a smile and leans back in his chair, tenting his fingers.

"Five or six," he repeats with a gentle smile. I always like it when I amuse people. He gets up out of his chair and reaches a hand across his desk.

"Thanks for comin' in, Mr. Bernardi. Too bad we had this little mix-up."

I don't take his hand. "I know what I saw, Sheriff."

"I know what you thought you saw," Claxton says withdrawing his hand. He comes around the desk and takes me by the elbow. "Easy enough to make a mistake, that time of night. Appreciate your stoppin' by."

"Doing my duty, Sheriff," I say, unable to get out of there fast enough.

"Also appreciate you people bringin' your movie to town. Lot of folks doin' really well havin' you here."

"Happy to oblige," I say.

I smile. He smiles. When I get outside, I blow my nose to get the stench of coverup out of my nasal passages. I hop in the car and direct Skeeter to find me a phone booth so I can look up Doctor Yardley's address. Skeeter goes me one better. He knows exactly where Yardley's office is and drives me there. The price I pay is having to listen to hit singles by the likes of Webb Pierce, Hank Snow and Loretta Lynn.

Yardley's office is in a private house at the edge of town. Skeeter accompanies me to the door since I gather that Yardley delivered him into the world some 18 years ago and because of that, Skeeter feels some sort of kinship. We ring the bell. No one answers. Puzzled, Skeeter knocks. After a moment, the door is opened by a scraggy grey-haired woman with dried up skin and noticeable scoliosis.

"Mornin', Miz Yardley. The Doc in?" Skeeter asks.

The old woman shakes her head.

"Gone to the barbecue," she says eyeing me suspiciously

"Don't know anything about any barbecue, ma'am." Skeeter tells her.

"Outside of town, Skeeter. Movie barbecue. Jeremy thinks he's a movie star. I tell him if any of his patients die while he's out there prancin' about like some fairy queen, Jesus will strike him down, yes, he will."

I head nod to Skeeter and he catches on.

"Well, thank you, Miz Yardley. You have a good day now."

We turn and head down the little gravel path to the street.

The old woman calls after us. "Send him home, Skeeter. He don't belong out there with all them hedonists!"

"I'll do that, ma'am!" Skeeter calls over his shoulder.

We pile into the car and take off. I shake my head.

"Wow,"I say, "if that's mother love, I want no part of it."

Skeeter looks over at me.

"No, sir, Mr. Bernardi. That's his wife."

I shake my head even harder. I wonder if Yardley drinks.

When we pull into the Reata parking area, the set is in chaos. A huge barbecue pit has been dug a couple of hundred yards in front of the main house and a steer is roasting on a spit. Nearly a hundred people, actors, extras and crew, are milling about as Stevens and Mellors design the next shot. Rock is chatting with a couple of the crew members, Elizabeth is sitting on a camp chair beneath a sturdy umbrella cooling herself with a stiff drink, and James Dean is sitting in the backseat of the Benedict convertible roadster, his booted feet up on the front seat backs and his Stetson pulled down over his eyes. If he's awake he gives no sign of it. Quite a distance away are the restraining ropes behind which stand several hundred townspeople and visitors, drinking in the glamour. It's a heady day for the people of Marfa.

I ask Skeeter to find Dr. Yardley and to bring him over to the craft services tent. I need to ask him a couple of questions. It won't take long. Skeeter heads for the milling crowd while I take off for the craft services tent where a few minutes ago, I spotted Willie standing by the entrance puffing on a cigarette.

When I enter the tent, Willie's nowhere to be seen. Maria Hernandez is whipping up a batch of tuna fish sandwiches while Flavia is standing over by the coffee urn in conversation with a good looking young man named Steve Keller, a local college kid working on the crew as a laborer until school starts up again in Austin. There are those who would not call giggling and outrageous flirtation conversation, but what do I know? I'm a 36 year old man with a non-existent love life and as far as I can remember, the last attractive young girl who batted her eyes at me was a waitress in a burger joint hoping for a five buck tip.

I grab a coffee mug and walk over to the urn. Steve is whispering delicately in her ear as I, Scrooge-like, move in to bust it up.

"Hate to interrupt the party," I say, "but I crave coffee."

Flavia steps back, slightly embarrassed.

Steve raises his hand apologetically. "Sorry, Mr. Bernardi. See you later, babe," he says to Flavia and slinks off as I start to pour. I smile at her.

"What happened to free time is for studying and no time for boys?" I say.

"Well, there are exceptions."

"Yes, I can see that." My eyes lower to her curvaceous bust line.

She has on a soft baby blue cashmere sweater and on her breast she is a wearing a very attractive pin. It's a black onyx heart bordered by tiny pearls and greek letters in gold embossed on the heart.

"That's new," I say. "Sigma Phi Epsilon."

She looks down at it and blushes.

"He was very insistent," she says.

"And we mustn't break the heart of a good upstanding fraternity boy."

She puts her finger to her lips.

"Don't say a word to Mom. She doesn't know what it means," she says.

"Do YOU know what it means?" I ask.

She smiles. "It means we'll both have a date on New Year's Eve."

"Well, in that case I will go to my death defending your secret, young damsel," I say.

"You know, Mr. Bernardi, sometimes you talk funny."

I wink at her and walk off with my mug of coffee just as Willie steps into the tent, fire in her eyes.

"Thanks for the wakeup call," she growls.

"The least I could do. You blasted me out of bed with a twenty-one gun salute before six o'clock."

"Are you saying I snore?" Willie asks.

"Does a tea kettle whistle?"

"I'm a heavy breather, that's all," Willie says defensively.

"I know heavy breathing, Willie—"

"I'll bet you do—"

"—and that ain't it. Much as I love you and need you, unless Tom Andre can find you a room of your own by this evening, you're on your way back to L.A."

"You can't fire me," she says indignantly.

"Sorry. I am not sleeping in the same room with you one more night."

"Then find me a place to bunk down."

Flavia has been watching this contretemps in dismay, looking at me, looking at Willie.

"Excuse me," she says.

We ignore her.

"You could always sleep in the lobby," I say.

"How about if you sleep in the lobby, boss? Listen, I've got a contract signed by your partner—" she says, voice raised.

"Force majeure. Act of God!" I respond matching her volume. "Not by me!"

"Excuse me!" Flavia shouts it loud enough to freeze us in place. We look over at her. "We have a spare bedroom," she says

"You're kidding," I say in disbelief.

"My brother Mike just left for boot camp at Ft. Sill. His room's going to be empty for the next ten weeks."

"Is that an offer?" I ask.

"Sure." She looks over at her mother. "Mama?"

"Ten dollars a night is what they're getting," Maria says flatly without looking up.

I grin. "It's a deal, senora, and God bless you," I say, totally relieved.

"De nada." She looks up with a smile.

Just then a man enters followed closely by Skeeter. He looks around with a big grin on his face.

"Somebody here call for a doctor?" he says jovially.

I walk over to him, my hand out.

"Dr. Yardley?"

"Mr. Bernardi?"

We shake.

"Let's find some place we can talk in private," I say to him and as I start to lead him out of the tent, I say over my shoulder, "You girls work out the sleeping arrangements."

Jeremy Yardley looks like Frank Capra's vision of a small town doctor. Short, grey haired, pot-bellied, looking a lot like Gene Lockhart. Today he's wearing fancy western duds with rattlesnake boots and a string tie with a silver clasp. I presume he's supposed to represent one of the local cattle ranchers.

"I hate to drag you away from the crowd, Doctor, but I'm pretty confused about the death of that young woman you autopsied last night."

Yardley shakes his head sadly.

"A darned shame, son. A pretty young thing like that. Breaks my heart. Did you know her?"

I shake my head."Not really. I shared a drink with her shortly before she died. Look, Doctor, here's the problem. You cited the time of death as between 8:00 and 9:00 the evening before her body was discovered."

"That's right."

"On what did you base that?"

"The usual indicators. Body temperature, contents of the stomach, lividity."

"Well, I don't know how it happened but your conclusion is off by about 4 or 5 hours. You see, around midnight the young lady and I were having drinks at a local bar. When she left shortly before one o'clock she was very much alive."

The expression on Yardley's face tightens and the twinkle fades from his eyes.

"You're mistaken," he says.

"Sorry, Doctor, I'm not and the bartender will back me up."

Now Yardley gets really steely-eyed.

"Son, I've been doing autopsies for nearly thirty years now and I don't make five hour mistakes in time of death. Seems to me you were getting drunk with some other girl and as for Pepe, he and his whole family and a band of angels can swear to anything they like, I made no mistake and I would take it kindly if you did not continue to repeat that slander to anyone else. Now, good day."

He turns and walks off and I stare after him, wondering what set off such a long-winded defensive denial. It isn't until I start to walk back into the tent that I realize that I had never mentioned the bartender's name.

CHAPTER FOUR

We've just picked up Willie's duffle bag at the hotel and now we're headed for Flavia's house located in the north end of town. The Hernandez family has been a fixture in Marfa since right after the war when Pedro came home from fighting the Japs on Okinawa. He could have taken the 52-50 government handout, fifty dollars a week for fifty two weeks, but instead he took his mustering out pay and put it down on a little store front on W. San Antonio Street and turned it into a Tex-Mex diner called Pecos Pete's Cafe. Six months later business was so good he bought the place next door, broke down the adjoining wall and added fifteen tables. By years end the little eatery had a reputation for the juiciest burgers and the spiciest tacos west of Dallas. When George Stevens came to Marfa to scout locations and to choose a catering service, the vote for Pete and Maria Hernandez was unanimous.

Skeeter pulls into the driveway of a neatly maintained two story house. The Hernandez home is a freshly painted white with blue trim and the landscaping consists of worry-free Texas shrubbery and cacti. We pile out of the car and head for the front door. Skeeter tries to help with Willie's duffle and gets an elbow in the ribs for his trouble. That's one of the things I like best about Willie. When she's at my side in a dicey situation, I don't have to worry that I'm not packing a gun. Willie is always up for anything.

We go inside and the girls head upstairs to brother Mike's empty bedroom. Skeeter goes into the kitchen to grab a glass of water and I give the place the once over. Everything is neat and well cared for. The furniture is heavy and stuffed and the wood is dark but the ambience is welcoming. Family pictures adorn the walls alongside crucifixes and icons of the Virgin Mary and other saints whose specialities escape me. I sit down on the sofa and that's when I spot it laying atop the coffee table next to a vase of wild flowers. I pick it up. It's the University of Texas yearbook for 1955.

Hopefully I start to leaf through it until I get to the section marked "Juniors". The photos are small and crammed onto the pages but they're plenty big enough for identification. Slowly I start to check out each one. It takes me several minutes but then I spot her. Stella Garcia. The clear skin, the abundant black hair, the flirtatious look in her eyes. Sheriff Claxton is wrong and so is Doctor Jeremy Yardley. Here is the girl who died sometime after one o'clock and not five hours earlier as Yardley claims. Now, as before when I left the Sheriff's office, I am vaguely troubled by the possibility of a coverup. I continue to leaf through the yearbook and when I get to the 'Sports' section, I find another photo of Stella. She's in a swimsuit at poolside with her arm around another young lady and they are mugging mercilessly for the camera. The caption reads, 'Stella Garcia and Lucinda Montoya, swim team mates forever." At that moment the girls come down the stairs. I wave to Flavia to come sit next to me on the sofa. She does and I turn the yearbook around so she can see clearly. I point my finger at Stella's picture. "Tell me about her," I say.

She peers down at the photo and starts to shake her head, then stops.

"That's the girl who was killed," she says.

I nod.

"Did you know her?"

"No, " Flavia says. "She's not from around here and I never ran into her on campus."

"You're sure?"

"Positive."

Willie leans in close.

"What is it, boss?" she asks. "Who is she?"

"Is that the girl from the bar?" Skeeter asks.

"It is," I say.

Neither Flavia nor Willie know about my encounter with Stella at the cantina the other night so I fill them in. I also tell them about the discrepancy in the time of death.

"Wow," Skeeter mutters, puzzled. Not half as much as I am.

"Flavia, of the young people who live here in Marfa, how many would you say are presently attending the university in Austin?"

She frowns.

"I don't know. Not a whole lot. Maybe a dozen or so. I don't think much more than that."

"She said she was supposed to meet a classmate at the cantina at midnight. A call comes in. She goes outside to wait and a few minutes later this young guy drives up in a new white Chevy Corvette. She gets in and they drive off. Mean anything to you?"

Flavia looks at me, then looks sharply toward Skeeter.

"Rowdy," Skeeter says quietly.

I look from one to the other.

"Who?"

"Rowdy Beddoe. He's the only guy in town I know drives a 'Vette," Skeeter says.

"Flavia, do you know this guy?"

"I've seen him on campus, but I don't know him. Not to speak to. He runs with a different crowd. Or he did. I think I remember someone telling me he flunked out. Or quit. One of the two."

I pick up the yearbook and scan the B's. I don't find his picture.

"Not here. What's he look like?" I ask.

Flavia shrugs.

"Kind of average. Not too tall. Nice build."

"Blonde hair?"

"That's right," she says.

"The guy in the 'Vette. He was blonde?" Skeeter asks.

I nod.

"Wow," Skeeter says again.

"Tell me about him," I say.

Skeeter shrugs. "Don't know all that much except his old man, J.W., is the richest rancher in the area. I heard Rowdy was booted out of a couple of prep schools back east and finished his high school right here in Marfa."

"I heard the same thing," Flavia says. "I don't think he studied much at UT. The guys he hung out with, they were keen on girls and booze. That was about it."

I sit quietly for a few moments and then I say, "I have to pay another call on the Sheriff."

Skeeter and I drop the girls back at the location and then we double back toward town. I'm edgy because I don't know what to expect from Sheriff Claxton. He's given me no reason to think he has an open mind which means he's either being very protective of an old friend or something much more sinister is in play. And since Rowdy Beddoe is the son of the richest man in the neighborhood, anything is possible. Second thoughts are beginning to cloud my thinking.

"Pull over," I say to Skeeter.

He does so.

"What's the problem, Mr. B.?" he asks.

"What do you know, if anything, about a man named Nick

Comstock?"

"Mr. Comstock? He taught me freshman English. That was right before he went to work for the newspaper."

"What kind of a guy is he?" I ask.

"A straight shooter. We all liked him a lot. Hated to see him go."

I nod thoughtfully.

"Okay, Skeeter, let's go to the newspaper office and see how straight this guy actually shoots."

Skeeter drives to the corner of Highland and Oak and pulls into the newspaper's parking lot. We both go inside in search of Nick Comstock. I keep Skeeter at my side to vouch for me if Comstock shows any reluctance to talk to me. We take the elevator to the second floor and find him in a little cubbyhole of a office, nervously chewing in the end of a pencil as he stares at a blank sheet of paper in his typewriter. I know the feeling.

"Mr. Comstock?" I say.

He looks up.

"That's me," he says.

I stick out my hand. "Joe Bernardi. I handle publicity for the movie."

He smiles. "I think you want Mrs. Peabody down at the end of the hall."

"I don't think so." I stare at him hard. He seems familiar. "Haven't I seen you over at Reata where they're filming the movie."

He nods. "I've stopped by a few times."

"Probably checking out Flavia Hernandez," says Skeeter's voice behind me. Comstock cranes his neck and a big smile crosses his face.

"Hey, Skeeter, how ya doin', fella?" he says.

"Real good, Mr. Comstock," Skeeter says. "Only one more year till she graduates."

"We're friends, Skeeter. Just friends. Pass that along to your juvenile pals."

"I'll do that and I sure hope it works out for you."

Comstock shakes his head in frustration and gives me a helpless look. "One day it was raining and I gave Flavia a lift to her house. He and his gang have been yammering on me ever since."

"Jealous," I say throwing him a wink. "Mind if I pull up a chair? I have a story that might interest you."

Comstock gestures to a chair in the adjoining cubicle which is unoccupied. I grab it and sit. Skeeter goes in search of a chair of his own.

"First off, I want to compliment you on your story in this morning's paper. Considering they gave you practically nothing to work with, you did a helluva job."

"Thanks," he nods. "Sure was tough getting much out of them."

"You mean the Sheriff."

"That's right. The Sheriff."

"What do you think of him?"

"The Sheriff?"

"That's right. The Sheriff?"

He regards me oddly.

"That's a strange question," Comstock says.

"I don't think so. I went to see him this morning, to tell him what I know about the death of that young woman, which is considerable. He wasn't really interested. What about you, Mr. Comstock? Are you interested?"

Skeeter returns with his chair and nudges himself into the conversation.

"I'm a reporter, Mr. Bernardi. Of course I'm interested."

"If I tell you the story will you print it?"

"Yes, if it's accurate and verifiable."

"I should warn you, it might not make you any friends."

"Making friends was not my purpose in taking this job."

"Very well," I say. "Grab a steno pad."

I start at the beginning and take him through it, step by step. My encounter with the young woman in the cantina witnessed by Pepe the bartender. The arrival of the white Corvette with the young blonde man at the wheel. The unexplainable discrepancy in the time of death as pronounced by Dr. Yardley and Sheriff Claxton's unquestioning support of his findings. The identification of Stella Garcia as the victim based on her photo in the yearbook. Finally, the conjecture that Rowdy Beddoe was the man behind the wheel of the Corvette.

Comstock looks up from his pad.

"You're suggesting that Rowdy Beddoe killed the girl and that the Sheriff and Doc Yardley are conspiring to cover it up."

"No, I'm presenting you with facts," I say. "In the end I don't know where they will lead."

"This identification of the girl—" He checks his notes. "Stella Garcia. You haven't shared this with Sheriff Claxton."

"No. It's my gut feeling that anything I present to the Sheriff will end up in a file drawer in a folder marked 'Forget About It'. That's why I started this conversation by asking you what you thought of the Sheriff."

Comstock looks down at his notes. He shakes his head.

"I can't believe Doc Yardley made that kind of mistake in the time of death."

"It was no mistake. An hour off. Maybe two. That's possible. Not five. Five is not a mistake," I say.

I watch him carefully as he licks his lips nervously and I feel sorry for him. He's a young, good looking guy, intelligent, eager, still idealistic. I've handed him a nuclear bomb and told him to defuse it and I can't blame him for being scared stiff.

"Look, Mr. Comstock— Nick. Maybe this is too much for you to handle. I wouldn't blame you for wanting to back away. Aside from a nagging desire to get the truth out, I have nothing at stake here. But this is your town. You have to live here and as I said, I have no clue where this will lead. It could end up getting very nasty."

Nick shrugs.

"If it does, it does. I didn't choose to become a reporter because I wanted to cover the Garden Club's monthly activities. He stands and puts out his hand. "I'll check this out. If it holds together, I'll write it. You're right about one thing, Mr. Bernardi, that young girl deserves better than she's been getting."

I shake his hand firmly. I'm surprised. Not a trace of sweat. I may be selling this young man short.

CHAPTER FIVE

I use Nick's phone to check in with Tom Andre at production headquarters at the hotel. It's now 4:30. He tells me the company will be shooting as late as 8:30 when they begin to lose the light. I decide I'd better get out there and make a token appearance. The dinner break's scheduled for 6:30 and maybe I can get a chance to chat with Elizabeth Taylor. Frankly I'd rather be at the Palace Theater tonight for the one-night showing of "A Place in the Sun", the movie in which every young teenage boy with raging hormones falls deeply in love with Elizabeth and learns to envy Monty Clift. Another reason why I like George Stevens. He directed it.

I'm feeling pretty chipper as we pull into the parking area several hundred yards from the ranch house. Everybody parks here but since the stars are ferried by Teamster drivers and the crew is transported by buses from the front entrance of the hotel, most of the cars belong to the extras recruited from the town as well as the dozens and dozens of onlookers. I feel as if a weight has been lifted from my back. If all goes well, Nick Comstock will blow the lid off Stella's murder tomorrow morning and the Sheriff will have to quit stonewalling and actually investigate her death. As for me. I've done my part and I have no intention of running around Marfa acting like a Nosy Norman when I have a movie to publicize.

And then as I get out of Skeeter's station wagon, I see it in the next row. The white Corvette with the red leather upholstery. Somewhere in that mass of humanity watching the filming is Rowdy Beddoe. Do I care? Not really. Am I a little curious? Maybe a bit. Am I going to track him down? Not a chance. Closing the book on Stella's death is someone else's problem.

Skeeter and I head for the set. The security guard recognizes us both and lets us pass. Skeeter peels off when he sees a friend from school. She's a dazzling blonde and looks good in leather pants. I look around for Willie and finally spot her over by the barbecue pit ripping off a few shots of Chill Wills who plays alcoholic Uncle Bawley. Stevens is busy giving instructions to the dolly crew so it'll be a while before the next shot. Willie sees me coming and breaks if off with Wills and comes to meet me with a grin on her face. At that moment, Steve Keller, one of the local college kids hired for the summer as laborers, walks past me and throws me a thumbs up and a smile. "Nice work," he says in passing. I stare after him. What the hell was that all about? I turn back as the D.P. Bill Mellors approaches.

"Good job, Joe. Really super. We're all with you a hundred per-cent," he says. I'm about to ask him what he's talking about when he and I hear his name being called and Stevens is waving him over toward the dolly track. "Scuse me. My master's voice," he says and turns back the way he came. Now I'm totally at sea as Willie marches up to me, still grinning.

"Did you know that old fella is the voice of Francis, the talking mule?" she says.

"Four movies worth," I say.

"What a nice old geezer," Willie says. "Kinda funny, too." "Speaking of funny, how come everybody's walking up to me and congratulating me? For what?"

"I guess they heard what you've been doing about Stella Garcia's murder."

"And how would they have heard about that?" I say, annoyed. "Probably Flavia. She's telling everybody. She's very proud of you, Joe. I'd say that door is wide open for you."

"Oh, for God's sake, Willie, she's a kid," I say.

"And a well developed one at that," Willie responds.

"And also one that needs to be silenced."

I start off for the craft services tent with Willie tagging along. She hurries to catch up.

"Oh, hey, I forgot to tell you," she says. "Bunny sends regards."

I stop dead in my tracks and face her. "What!"

"She called the hotel this morning. Actually she woke me up."

"You answered the phone in my hotel room? Oh, Lord."

"It's okay, Joe. When I explained who I was and what I was doing there, she understood completely."

"Oh, I'll bet she did," I say, aghast at the thought of what was probably going on in Bunny's mind. Given six choices about any situation ranging from best to worst possible outcome, Bunny will choose number seven. "I don't suppose she left a number."

"No, but she did say she'd try to call back this evening."

"Did she sound like she meant it?"

"Not really," Willie admits.

Oh, great, I think, as I sink into a funk. The good news is she's not dead, not in a hospital, and apparently not hurt. The bad news is, there will be no explaining Willie. I walk into the tent bent on requesting a glass of hemlock and knowing I will have to settle for a Nehi.

Flavia is standing by the sandwich table, leaning away from a man whose back is to me. His hand is resting on her shoulder and he is much too close to be merely ordering a chicken salad sandwich. Flavia sees me enter and her expression changes from one of panic to relief. "Oh, here he is now," she says. The man turns. He's young and he's blonde and he has a cocky half-smile on his face which I am to learn is a perpetual expression. He wears no name tag but there's no doubt. This is Rowdy Beddoe.

"You Bernardi?" he sneers.

"Me Bernardi. You Rowdy," I answer politely.

"You've been talking about me. I don't like it."

He takes a menacing step in my direction.

"I don't blame you," I say.

"Is that supposed to be some kind of smart answer?"

"Oh, no," I say, modestly. "I'm not smart enough to say something really clever like that."

He stares at me bewildered, unsure whether I have mocked or insulted him. I've known guys like Rowdy all my life. Slow upstairs, muscle bound elsewhere and incapable of dealing in argument. His solution to a dispute invariably involves fisticuffs.

"You're saying I killed that girl."

"Stella Garcia?"

"Is that her name?"

"You know it is," I say. "You were supposed to meet her at the cantina at midnight. You didn't show up until almost one o'clock."

"I was never there."

"Of course you were. I saw you."

"You're a liar."

"I don't think so. You drove up in your Corvette, she got in the car, and you drove off. I don't know what happened after that but I can guess."

Again, he steps toward me angrily, face reddening, his fists balling.

"Listen, old man—" he starts to say.

"I am not an old man. Age is a relative thing, Rowdy. I'm actually on the young side of middle age. That makes you a pipsqueak."

You may be wondering why I am so anxious to get my head knocked off. It's because Willie has her camera at the ready and is itching to document an assault on my person by this cretin. It will certainly spice up Nick Comstock's front page story in tomorrow's edition of the paper. I bruise easily but nonetheless I like the tradeoff. Now I have mentioned that Rowdy is slow but he's not that slow. He spots Willie out of the corner of his eye and his bloodlust cools to room temperature. The fists unclench and he backs off a step.

"I'm gonna sue your ass, buddy, you just see if I don't," Rowdy growls with great conviction and then storms from the tent.

I look over at Willie who is a study in dejection. She really wanted to snap that picture. I look at Flavia who is wide-eyed and open-mouthed. The drama on this location is not restricted to what is being filmed out by the barbecue pit.

"Flavia, I know you meant no harm and what's done is done but from now on, could we just not discuss the subject?"

"I'm very sorry, Mr. Bernardi," she says.

I put my finger to my lips and smile. She nods and smiles back. Willie and I grab a couple of sodas and walk outside where we run smack dab into a welcoming committee. Steve Keller, the college kid, is in the forefront of a group of a dozen or so other students picking up summer money before going back to school and they are all applauding. I guess when they heard the shouting coming from within, they were reluctant to enter and interrupt the proceedings, but they certainly seem pleased by the way things turned out.

"Well said, Mr. Bernardi," Steve says and his gang backs him up with a lot of buzz and whistles. "The boys and I didn't know that girl but we sure as hell know all about Rowdy Beddoe. He's been pulling crap like this for years. Nice to see him take it up the butt." More shouts of approval from the boys.

"Thanks, guys, but it's over and done with," I say.

"Maybe so, " Steve says, "but just as a reminder of the day, we talked to the horse wranglers and they left a little present for Rowdy on the front seat of his fancy Corvette."

"The horse wranglers, you say?"

"The horse wranglers," Steve says solemnly.

I look at Willie who is fighting back a huge guffaw.

"A token of your esteem?"

"Most appropriately so," says the skinny bespectacled kid standing to Steve's left. More laughter.

"Okay, boys, enough is enough. Don't get yourselves fired. He's not worth it."

Willie and I push past them headed for the set. Their enthusiasm is unabated and I feel kind of like a folk hero. Several of the young men clap me on the shoulder as I brush by them and I acknowledge them with a smile. Of course, what they have done is wrong. Tasteless and terribly juvenile. I wish I'd thought of it.

I go in search of Elizabeth and reach her just in time to say hello before the assistant director calls "lunch" which in this case is dinner. I needn't have worried. She invites me to join her in her trailer while we eat. Her stand-in volunteers to get us plates while we make ourselves comfortable, me with a beer and she with an RC Cola she keeps in her mini refrigerator.

Just as I remember her she is warm and gracious and genuinely interested in what I've been up to the past couple of years. She asks about Bunny although she doesn't remember her name ("that pretty little thing that worked for the Hollywood Reporter") and wonders what it's like to work without Jack Warner to deal with every minute of the day. She even thanks me for arranging transportation to Quebec City, Canada, for a short visit with Monty Clift on the set of "I Confess". Even though she was unable to come, still she remembers. This is one classy lady. We chat about the picture, her joy at working with George Stevens once again, her delight at co-starring with Rock Hudson. "Such a kind and gentle man" she says. She pointedly doesn't mention James Dean and so I ask her about him. Her expression becomes thoughtful. A nice young man, she says. And? She shakes her head. Not to be quoted, she says, but it is sometimes difficult playing a scene with him. He's very mannered. Prima donna? I ask. No, she says, he's sincere. It's not ego. It's the way he was trained. It's a technique he's comfortable with. She smiles. It's just that some of the rest of us don't share that comfort. I promise that her opinion will be our little secret.

Much too soon the assistant director knocks on the trailer door. Dinner break is over. Miss Taylor is wanted on the set. I walk her over to the barbecue pit and we say our au revoirs. Some time in the next few days I'll sit down with her and do a full scale interview. Willie will snap dozens of photos. Of one thing I am sure. The world cannot get enough of Elizabeth Taylor and who am I to disagree?

I rescue Skeeter from the blonde in the tight leather pants and obviously unwilling, he drives me back to the hotel where I have an important phone call to make before the day disappears completely. Once in my room I check for messages. Jack Warner. He'll keep. My partner Bertha Bowles. She, too, will keep. Phineas Ogilvy, the entertainment editor for the L.A. Times. Strange. Phineas is listed as a local number. No matter. It's still three for three on my wait list. I check my watch. 7:45. That makes it 6:45 on the coast. I take a chance and give the hotel operator a number to call. I'm rewarded a few minutes later when Ginger Tate comes on the line. Ginger, who still works for the Hollywood Reporter, has been and maybe still is Bunny's best friend.

"You're working late," I say.

"A lot going on," she says. "What's up, Joe?"

"I'm in trouble, Ginger. I need help. Do you have Bunny's phone number?"

"I do, but I won't give it to you. Strict orders."

"Don't want it," I say, "but I need you to call her for me." I tell her about the morning call to my room answered by Willie and the shortage of rooms that forced her to bunk in with me on an emergency basis. "Bunny is probably assuming the worst but it's not true. Willie's my photographer. Our relationship is strictly business. She has no interest in men and if she did, I'd be at the bottom of her list."

"I'm not going to tell her all that."

"I don't expect you to. Just have her call me here at the hotel. I'll stay up to midnight if I have to. Just have her call." I give Ginger the phone number, thank her, and hang up. I look at the list in my hand and slip it into the middle drawer of my desk. No call backs tonight. I don't want to jam up my line and miss her call. I flip on the television set and half-watch a parade of inane programs. When 'Broadway Open House' comes on, my patience has run out. It's past midnight and I'm a wreck. I turn off the TV, strip down to my skivvies and slip under the covers. I spend a fitful night which does not include a lot of sleep.

CHAPTER SIX

I've ordered breakfast in my room because I can no longer abide the crowded dining room unless I eat very late which I hate doing. I also like room service because they provide the morning newspaper. I am looking forward to reading Nick Comstock's story undisturbed and as soon as my waiter leaves, I grab the paper and turn to page one. The banner headline and the story above the fold concerns a woman who gave birth to twin boys in the back seat of a taxi on the way to the hospital. She immediately christened them Hack, as in Stan Hack, and Cab, as in Cab Calloway. Makes sense to me. The by-line belongs to someone named Priscilla.

I check below the fold. Gas prices have soared to 24 cents a gallon at the local Sinclair station. The city council is poised to investigate. I turn the page and then I keep turning until I get to the obituaries at the back of the paper next to a full page ad for the local Ford dealer who is offering a spanking new 1956 fully loaded Fairlane 2-door hardtop for just $2199. This is 1955. Why is this man selling 1956 cars? Has he got anything sharp in a 1957 model? Just asking.

Something is terribly wrong. There is no explosive story about Stella Garcia's murder. Not even a little throwaway at the bottom of page 27. I call the hotel operator and ask her to get me the news-paper office and when I'm connected I ask for Nick Comstock. I don't really expect to speak to him, not at this hour of the morn-ing, so I am astonished when he comes on the line. He sounds half dead and I have a suspicion he's gone through hell.

"Nick, it's Joe Bernardi."

"Jesus, man, I am so sorry."

"What happened?"

"My editor spiked the story. Said I couldn't back it up."

"Did you talk to Pepe the bartender?" I ask.

"I couldn't, Joe. The place was closed. No one's around. I think he's left town."

"What?"

"I went by at five o'clock and the 'Closed' sign was posted in the window. I went back around eight o'clock and the sign was still there but someone had scrawled 'Family Emergency' on it."

"Not good, Nick," I say.

"It sure isn't," he says. "And it's not just the lack of proof that's got my boss spooked. I mean the whole idea of going up against the Sheriff and Doc Yardley and especially J.W. Beddoe, I think he's scared shitless."

"I understand," I say. "Nick, don't lose that story. I don't think it's dead yet. I'll get back to you."

"I'll be here," he says.

I hang up and rummage around in the desk drawer for the slip of paper with my phone messages on it. It's much too early to call Jack Warner or Bertha on the coast but Phineas is a local number. The hotel operator calls it for me through her switchboard.

A familiar voice answers the phone.

"Phineas," it says in a basso profundo that Ezio Pinza would envy.

"On the road, you goldbrick? What happened to your gout?" I say.

"Ah, Joseph, old top, what a delight to hear your voice. The gout flared up last month when it appeared I might have to fly to North Dakota for the Bismarck Film Festival. Just as the Festival concluded my gout disappeared. With Hudson, Taylor and Dean in the offing, I do not expect a recurrence."

"And what is this phone number? Where are you staying?"

"With Vera."

"And who the hell is Vera?" I ask.

"My first wife. When I was unable to book hotel accommodations, Vera graciously offered to put me up for a few days."

"I don't remember Vera," I say.

"Nor should you," Phineas says. "It was twenty two years and one hundred and fifteen pounds ago, old top. I'm happy to report that she, unlike me, is lovelier than ever."

Phineas, who writes about the movies for the L.A. Times, is a flamboyant figure with a Mensa mind who travels in all the right circles. Most people believe he's homosexual. I don't. Vera is the first of his three wives. I've met the other two. They are knockouts.

"When shall we break bread?" he asks.

"I've just broken it. How about lunch on the set at one o'clock? I'll introduce you around."

"How disappointing. I was going to suggest that I introduce YOU around." I decide not to respond as I have yet to get the last word from this man, ever.

"I'm so grateful," I say. "Do you have wheels?"

"I do, Vera uses her sizable alimony checks to purchase multiple cars."

"And do you have a driver's license?"

"I was told it was unnecessary in Texas as long as I carry a shotgun in the front seat but yes, I do."

"Then meet me at the production office in the Hotel Paisano in a half hour and after we run a short errand, you can drive us out to the location."

"I am at your service, old top."

I hang up and wolf down the rest of my now-cold breakfast. I dress quickly and hurry downstairs where I leave word that Skeeter can have the day off. I find a message in my cubby hole. Willie is sleeping in this morning and will catch up with me at the Reata later on. I ask Tom's assistant, Olivia, to pass the word to Skeeter and then walk over to the coffee urn to pour a cup of joe as I wait for Phineas. I catch sight of an elegantly dressed man in three piece grey flannel who enters and looks around, then approaches Olivia and asks a question. She points at me and he nods with a snake-like smile. Why is it that guys who dress like out-of-work European royalty are always bad news?

"Mr. Joseph Bernardi?" he asks.

"Yes."

He whips his business card from one of his vest pockets and presents it with a flair.

"Marcus Gallantree, attorney at law," he says.

"Ah," I say, apropos of nothing.

"I represent Leland Beddoe."

I nod. "That would be young Rowdy."

"It would be. Young Mr. Beddoe is rightfully upset about the scurrilous accusations you have made about him in connection with the death of that unfortunate young woman."

"I made no accusations, Mr. Gallantree. I merely told some friends that I had seen Stella Garcia get into a car with Mr. Beddoe around one in the morning a few hours before she was killed."

"Slanderous, Mr. Bernardi. The woman was killed between eight and nine o'clock at least four hours earlier."

"And were you there with her when and where she was killed?"

"Of course not."

"Well, I was there when she drove off in Rowdy Beddoe's

Corvette so my testimony is eyewitness while yours is conjecture and mighty faulty conjecture at that."

"We have only your word that such a thing happened," Gallantree says, trying to keep the sneer out of his voice.

"No, we have Pepe the bartender," I say.

"Do we? Then let's produce him and we can settle this matter immediately."

"Excellent idea!" I chortle ebulliently. "He'll be calling me at noon today. We arranged to maintain contact in this matter in case he was suddenly drawn out of town by, oh, say a family emergency."

I'm bluffing, of course, but I wanted to see what effect this little white lie would have on the patrician Mr. Gallantree. A profound one, I should think, as I watch the blood drain from his face.

"If this Pepe gentleman is calling to verify your story, sir, this means only that I have two liars on my hands and I will deal with you both appropriately."

"I smell lawsuit," I say.

"Indeed you do," Marcus Gallantree says.

"I'm delighted. Having talked to a great many locals who have known Mr. Beddoe for most or all of his life, I doubt I could find twelve men good and true who would believe young Leland if he insisted that the Rio Grande was a river."

"We shall see," Gallantree says.

"Yes, we will, and when I countersue, with the backing of Jack Warner, I am likely to be awarded enough in damages to retire in comfort because, you see, sir, I am very sure that the good people of Marfa have been waiting a long time to stick it to your arrogant, cold blooded weasel of a client. I may be wrong, but as you say, we shall see."

Gallantree glares at me hard for several very long seconds before he finally says, "We shall meet again, Mr. Bernardi." Then he turns and strides from the room.

I sit back down and sip my coffee. I don't know whether to be enthused or frightened. The conspiracy widens and if there had been the least doubt in my mind about Rowdy Beddoe's guilt, it has been wiped away by the appearance of this high priced shyster in his three-piece suit. This is mitigated by the reality that I am most likely at war not only with the Sheriff but also the most powerful man for miles around. There's no doubt this situation could quickly become hazardous to my health.

Ten minutes later Phineas arrives, conservatively dressed in a mustard-colored suit, forest green ascot around his neck, and rattle-snake boots on his feet. Atop his head he is wearing a deerstalker cap, identical to the one often sported by Sherlock Holmes.

I look at him in disbelief.

"You needn't have dressed down just for me, old friend," I say to him.

He waves his hand dismissively.

"I didn't want to be late so this is just something I slapped together."

I shrug. "In a totally dark room, I presume. You'll hardly be noticed. And what sort of vehicle did you arrive in? A school bus?"

No, it isn't a school bus, it's a brand new Bentley S-1 right hand drive sedan, ebony in color with a burled dashboard and grey calf-skin upholstery. A dozen people are inspecting it closely. I fear if we don't leave immediately, they'll be joined by a dozen more. We clear away the crowd and a few moments later we are headed out of the hotel parking lot. Phineas apologizes for arriving in the Bentley but Vera adamantly refused to lend him either the Lincoln Capri or her brand new Cadillac Coupe de Ville. Now I am beginning to understand why Phineas is always short of cash. Vera plus two more ex-wives clawing at his assets? How much can one man afford?

"Left at the corner," I tell him.

"I was told the location is straight out Route 90."

"It is but we have a stop to make."

Ten minutes later I have guided him to the parking lot of Pepe's ramshackle cantina at the edge of town. On the way I have related the short version of the murder and Rowdy Beddoe's probable involvement in it. Phineas takes it all in with enthusiasm. If there's one thing he loves it's a good murder.

Even before we get out of the car, I can see the CLOSED sign tucked in the front window. I walk over and inspect it. Scrawled at the bottom of the sign is the notation 'Family Emergency'.

I go to the front door and bang on it loudly. No response. I repeat myself, pounding even more loudly. Phineas thinks perhaps I have lost my senses until I tell him that I am sure I saw a curtain flutter in an upstairs window just as we drove up. I back away from the door and start shouting loudly at the window where I spotted the flutter. Still no response. Phineas grabs my elbow and signals me to silence and then starts to shout in that deep authoritative voice a lengthy tirade in Spanish which he speaks fluently. I catch words like "policia" and "dinero" and "muerto". Only the dead can fail to hear him.

He stops and we wait and a minute or so later, the door opens and a heavy set Hispanic woman with Indian features anxiously peers out at us. Phineas moves to her, takes her hand and kisses her fingers and then starts to speak to her gently. She responds. He smiles. She nods, He nods. She smiles. He reaches for his wallet and hands her a couple of bills. She nods gratefully. He kisses her fingers again and then as she goes back inside, shutting the door, he returns to me.

"You have been done in by the opposition," Phineas says. "Wednesday evening a man showed up after closing time. Neither Pepe nor the wife had ever seen him before. He claimed to be from Guadalajara, a good friend of Pepe's mother, who is very ill in the local hospital. The church had raised money so that Pepe could return to be at his mother's side at this critical time. The man handed Pepe an envelope containing a thousand dollars in cash and the following morning Pepe was on a bus to El Paso where he would pick up a Mexican bus to Guadalajara."

I nod glumly.

"The old sick-mother-in-Guadalajara trick," I say resignedly.

"Precisely," Phineas replies.

I sigh, both disappointed and frustrated.

"There was a favor I was going to ask you once I got Pepe to back up my story—"

"Yes," Phineas says without hesitation.

"Yes, what?" I snap at him.

"You were going to ask me if I would write up this whole sordid affair in tomorrow's column for the Times and my answer, of course, is yes. If this local paper won't tell the truth about what's going on, I will. I'll also make sure that a hundred copies of the paper are bundled aboard the early morning train. You and I will then distribute them very judiciously and very publicly and then stand back and await the howls of despair from the conspirators. Tell me, old top, is that what you had in mind?"

I grin.

"Close enough, old top," I say.

CHAPTER SEVEN

hings are progressing slowly on the set. Stevens is covering the welcoming party from every angle, over and over and over. It's his style. The more raw footage he has the better the scenes can be edited. Or that's the theory. The drawback is the toll it takes on the cast and crew, knowing that 90% of what is being shot will be thrown away. Nonetheless no one complains. Stevens is the boss and Stevens makes remarkably good films. However it is now a certainty that the filming of this scene will bleed over into Saturday.

Phineas makes the rounds during setups and becomes the hit of the shoot. Cast and crew alike are delighted by his good humor and endless repertoire of stories. Rock and Elizabeth are old friends. Dean has just made his acquaintance and it's obvious he, too, has been charmed by the old hamhock. I look around for Willie. No sign of her yet. I check with Flavia who says Willie was still asleep when Flavia left the house early this morning. I notice that Flavia isn't her usual upbeat self this morning but I ascribe it to feminine indispositions. I grab a soda and head for the set. I turn when I hear my name.

"Yo, Mr. Bernardi!"

Steve Keller is walking toward me accompanied by the skinny

bespectacled kid and a beefy young man in a shirt without sleeves that shows off his considerable physique. I make it a point to introduce myself. His name is Big George. The skinny kid is Wally.

"I think, that is, we think that you ought to know, Rowdy was hanging around here this morning," Steve says.

I swivel around, looking for Rowdy.

"He left about twenty minutes ago," Steve continues.

I shrug. "It's a free country, I guess."

"He was sniffing around after Flavia," Steve says. "I say it's not that free. I told him to leave or I'd beat the crap out of him. So he left."

"Okay," I say.

"Is it? I mean, is it okay? I really hate the bastard, especially after what he did to that other girl—"

"That hasn't been proved, Steve," I break in.

"Yeah, but we all know what happened and we also know there's no sense in waiting around for the courts to deal with him because that isn't going to happen. Or am I wrong about that?"

"Probably not," I say.

"I just hate the idea of him coming anywhere near Flavia. We all like her a lot. She's really a great gal."

"We should beat the hell out of him," skinny Wally says.

"Only if you want to spend a year or two in a Texas prison, Wally," I say. "Assault is a crime and in this town assault against someone named Beddoe could get you into much deeper trouble than a stretch in prison."

"We can't just do nothin'," Big George grunts.

"Yes, you can, George," I say, "Because you can't jeopardize your future." This is not what the boys want to hear but I think deep down they know I'm right. I continue. "But I tell you what I'll do. I'll talk to security. I've got enough clout around here to see that a guard is posted near Flavia around the clock."

Steve brightens. "Yeah, that would be good."

"I'll see to it," I say. "Meanwhile, you guys keep your noses clean."

They promise to do so and go off feeling a lot better. I look around for the head of security. Fifteen minutes later I find him. His name is Sheffield and he's ex-Shore Patrol. He's also a lifelong Marfa resident and he knows all about Rowdy Beddoe. He agrees completely with the need to watch over Flavia. By now Willie has arrived and I fill her in. Her eyes light up. She's ready to do her part when Flavia's in transit or at home. I warn Willie to be careful. Rowdy has proven to be a very dangerous young man. In response, Willie unzips the camera bag hanging over her right shoulder and allows me to peer inside. I see a dozen rolls of film, assorted flash-bulbs, a light meter, various lens filters, and a .38 caliber Walther PPK with four extra clips. I look up at her and don't even bother to ask if she knows how to use it. The glint of anticipation in her eyes is all I need to know.

By three o'clock Phineas and I are back at the hotel. We've stopped by the newspaper office and picked up Nick Comstock's rejected story and now Phineas is at a desk, reading and re-writing and putting together his own version of the murder of Stella Garcia. He'll phone this in to the Times' desk by six o'clock in plenty of time to meet the deadline for tomorrow's edition. Meanwhile I'm on the phone at the next desk talking with the registrar's office at the University of Texas in Austin.

"What was that name again?" the woman asks.

"Lucinda Montoya."

"And you are?"

For the third time I give her my name and for the third time I tell her I am not a relative but a friend. Lucinda is the young varsity swimmer who was mugging with Stella for the camera in the UT yearbook.

"I'm not sure I should give out this information," she says.

"I understand, ma'am, but this is an emergency. We're here in Marfa dealing with the murder of Miss Montoya's best friend. Lucinda needs to be told about it by someone who cares before she hears it on a radio broadcast."

There is a long silence and finally the woman relents and gives me the phone number.

"And that is in Texas?" I ask.

"Yes. Fort Davis."

Fort Davis. That's unbelievably good news. Fort Davis is a mere twenty miles from here, straight north on Route 17. I had planned to chat with Lucinda on the phone, not the best approach considering the subject matter. Now I have a chance to speak to her face to face. I ask for Lucinda's street address and after another minute or two of agonizing, the lady gives it to me.

As soon as I hang up, I turn to Phineas.

"Put down the pencil. We need to take a trip," I say.

"Dear boy, can you not see that I am in the arms of my Muse?"

"You mean you're writing."

"Of course I'm writing. Didn't I just say that?"

"Well, it'll have to keep. We need to drive to Fort Davis."

"Is that like the Alamo?"

"No. It's a town. I need to query someone who lives there."

"Then query away. I must finish this column and get it off to Los Angeles post haste." He picks up the car keys and tosses them at me.

"Vera might not approve," I say.

"Vera does not approve of anything except the Christian Science Monitor and even that is losing its mystique."

I get to my feet.

"I'll be back in a couple of hours."

"Take your time, old top. I may still be at this when you return." He waves me away. "Shoo, shoo!" he says.

I shoo.

It takes a few minutes to get used to the Bentley's right hand drive but when I do, it comes naturally. The car is powerful and the ride is smooth and shortly before four o'clock I pull up in front of the Montoya residence in the heart of Fort Davis. It's a small house in a modest neighborhood but it is well cared for and appears to be newly painted.

Lucinda's mother answers the doorbell and at first she's wary until I mention Stella. Yes, Stella Garcia. She and Lucinda have been friends for many years starting back ten years ago before Stella and her family moved away to San Antonio. She tells me that Lucinda is down at the town's sports center doing laps in the swimming pool. She's on a sports scholarship at the university, what the kids call a "free ride". Without it she'd have to drop out of school and her Mom assures me that Lucinda has no intention of letting that happen. I don't mention Stella's death. I'll leave that to Lucinda. I get directions and take my leave. Fort Davis is not a big town and the sports center is close by.

Like Marfa, the temperature here in Fort Davis is hot and dry. When I walk into the sports center it's hot and humid. There is no air conditioning that I can detect and almost immediately I start to sweat. To the left there's a check-in desk and beyond that I see a weight room and a glimpse of a basketball court. The sounds of male voices and a bouncing ball reverberate from floor to ceiling. To the right, on the other side of a paneled glass wall, is an olympic sized swimming pool. I open a door and walk in to even more echoed noise and stifling humidity. A dozen or so kids are splashing and roughhousing in the shallow end. At the deep end a solitary female is swimming back and forth from side to side, cutting through the water in perfect form. I lean back against the wall, watching her, dreading what I have come to tell her. After few more minutes she edges off toward a ladder and climbs out of the pool.

She walks over to a nearby bench and slips into a terry cloth robe as I approach her, drenched in perspiration.

"Miss Montoya?"

She looks up at me curiously.

"Yes."

"My name is Joseph Bernardi. I've just driven up from Marfa. Is there someplace we could talk?"

Now she's suspicious.

"About what?" she asks.

"Stella."

And now I see fear. She looks around and spots a nearby table. She gestures to it and then walks over and sits down. I sit down next to her as she searches my face. She's not unattractive but she's plain looking. Her body is all muscle with no soft curves and she boasts shoulders that an NFL linebacker would envy.

"It's bad news, isn't it?" she says.

I nod. I reach over and take her hand in mine and when I do I feel her stiffen. I tell her quickly and quietly and as gently as I can but there is no easy way to tell a twenty year old that her best friend is dead. Twenty year olds are immortal. Death is an alien concept. It is the disease of old people.

For a few moments she is silent and then she asks, "Accident?"

I say no.

"That son of a bitch," she says angrily.

"Who?" I say.

"His name is Rowdy Beddoe. She told me she was going to confront him. I warned her not to. Rowdy is a psychopath. He does what he wants, when he wants to. He doesn't care who he hurts. How did it happen?"

"She was strangled."

She shudders slightly and looks away.

"Have they arrested him?"

"No."

A wry smile crosses her lips. "No, of course they haven't."

"You said she was going to confront him. About what?"

She shakes her head.

"Nothing important."

"Maybe it is," I say. "Aside from Rowdy I'm probably the last person who saw her alive. We were having a drink at this bar. She was flirting with me outrageously. Out of anger, maybe. Or bitterness. I played along even though we were just kidding each other."

"Yeah, that was Stella. She could be a great kidder."

"She said something odd to me. Like, you can't get me in trouble. Not now. I guarantee it." I await a reaction. I don't get it. She watches the kids in the shallow end of the pool. Finally I come right out with it. "Lucinda, was she pregnant?"

"What's the difference?"

"The difference is motive. He'd have had a reason."

Now she actually laughs but the laugh is bitter.

"Oh, yes, he had a reason. It wouldn't do for some lily white rancher's boy to have himself a half-Mex kid. Oh, not that. I told her. I told her to stay away from him. She wouldn't listen. All of them, they don't listen. They get lucky and find their way out of the barrio and then they think, sure, I can have it all. The good life. The rich life. The gringo's life. I tell them, the gringos don't see it that way. Like shouting in a twister. Nobody hears. Nobody listens." She looks me in the eye. "Yes, she was pregnant. Three months."

"No question?"

"No question."

Ten minutes out of Fort Davis on my way back to Marfa, my mind is awhirl with what I have learned. One thing I am sure of. Rowdy Beddoe killed Stella Garcia. I had been missing only a strong motive. Her pregnancy fills in that blank. My eye falls on the petrol gauge. To me it looks like the needle is resting on E. This is not good since I have no idea what sort of reserve the tanks carry, if any, and I'm in no mood to be stuck out here on this desolate wind blown, dust choked road. Happily, luck is on my side. Up ahead I spot a Texaco station and I breathe a little sigh of relief when I pull up to one of the two pumps. A white haired old man in rumpled pants and a soup stained shirt emerges from the office carrying a clipboard.

"Howdy," he says.

"Howdy," I reply.

He copies my license plate number down on the clipboard and smiles again.

"When you're finished pumpin', pay inside," he says and then walks back toward the office.

It takes me a minute to find the gas cap but when I do I start to pump. Just then a truck pulls into the station. It doesn't pull forward to the second pump but stops directly behind me. The truck's a three or four year old white Ford F1 with two men in front. The driver stays put. The other man gets out and approaches me. I notice he wears a cowboy hat and a revolver in a holster on his hip but I don't see a badge on his shirt. He gets really close and stares at me with a mirthless smile.

"Do I know you?" I say to him.

"Not yet you don't," he replies in an easy Texas drawl tipping his hat back slightly on his head.

"Something I can do for you?" I try again.

'You sure can," he says. "You can drive us both to Marfa."

I look back at the truck.

"Seems to me you've already got wheels."

"That's T.J. He's gonna follow us in."

"You know I'd just as soon ride by myself, if you don't mind."

"I do mind, Mr. Benard, so shut the fuck up, hang up the pump and get behind the wheel." The smile has never left his face but his right hand has dropped to the grip of his revolver.

I'm no fool. I do as I'm told. I stop pumping and start around to the front of the car.

"The name's Bernardi. Not Benard, Bernardi," I tell him.

"Do I look like I give a flying fuck?" he says as he gets into the passenger side. When I'm behind the wheel, he tells me to drive. I tell him I haven't paid for the gas. He looks at me like I must be the missing link. I drive. As I tool down the highway, I look in my mirror. The truck is close behind me.

On the way back to Marfa we don't say much. He doesn't give his name and I don't ask. Twice he tells me I must be the dumbest driver that God ever created. He and T.J. followed me all the way to Fort Davis from Marfa and I had no clue they were there. I apologize for being so stupid. I promise it won't happen again.

We're about a mile out of Marfa when my traveling companion tells me to turn right onto a dirt road marked "Private". I do and instantly I'm kicking up enough dirt to fill a dozen good sized pot holes. The Bentley wobbles and sways in the ruts of this ill-maintained road but even at that, the ride is relatively smooth. And suddenly there it is, a tall sign overhanging the road. "J.W. Beddoe- Private- Trespassers Will Be Shot".

Immediately I begin to wonder about my status. Unwelcome guest? Kidnap victim? Trespasser? The options are limited and I don't like any of them. Especially that last one.

CHAPTER EIGHT

.W. Beddoe's ranch house is an unimpressive one story stucco building that sprawls haphazardly in every direction. Just a hunch but I get the feeling it started out modestly and was added to every year or so as conditions dictated. The fictional Reata as envisioned by the movie's art director is a symbol of excess. J.W.'s spread is at the other end of the scale. A humble abode, incongruous for the most powerful man in the county.

I park next to a cream-colored Caddy Coupe de Ville with the license plate "ATTY" and get out of the car. The two bozos lead me into the house through the front door without knocking. Obviously I'm expected. Just off the foyer is very large room with a high ceiling. Heavy overstuffed pieces of furniture are everywhere alongside oversized cocktail tables. The floor is covered with thick carpeting. The walls are festooned with the remains of various animals ranging from longhorn cattle to elk, moose, deer and even sheep. There is a fire in the hearth which is situated across from a substantial and well stocked bar at which three men are sitting. Two I recognize.

Marcus Gallantree, elegant attorney at law, gets off his bar stool and approaches me with a smile on his face, hand extended in a gesture of camaraderie. He seems to have forgotten the acrimonious tenor of our last meeting.

"Good evening, Mr. Bernardi, so nice of you to join us," he says. As if I had a choice. I shake his hand out of politeness but grip only his cold bony fingers.

"I could hardly resist such a persuasive invitation," I say.

"Come say hello to J.W.," he says as he leads me to the bar.

J.W. Beddoe hefts himself off his barstool and reaches out his hand. We shake. This time the grip is warm and firm and the smile on Beddoe's face seems genuine.

"Welcome to my home, Mr. Bernardi. I apologize for the manner in which you were brought here but I was afraid that a simple invitation would be ignored."

"And you'd have been right," I say.

He laughs. "I usually am."

Such politeness. So many smiles. I feel like the guest of honor at a gathering of cannibals.

"Can I offer you a drink?" J.W. asks

"Beer's fine," I say.

J.W. signals to one of my abductors. "T.J., a cold beer for my guest," he says.

He's not big, this most powerful man in the county, not Rock Hudson big, but he's stocky and thick through the chest and at an inch or two under six feet, I suspect that even at age fifty or so he can take care of himself. He has a broad open face and a likable smile and a little of the Irish in his speech. I decide for the moment to keep an open mind about him.

"By the way, I believe you know the Sheriff," he says indicating Claxton who is sitting by himself at the end of the bar, smoking a cigarette and working on a highball.

"I do," I say, waving in his direction. Claxton lazily waves back, a model of total disinterest. That highball may not be his first of the evening.

"Why don't we sit down where it's more comfortable, Mr. Bernardi," J.W. says, pointing toward a nearby sofa flanked by a couple of easy chairs.

"Why not?" I say as the one called T.J. hands me a beer in a glass mug. Gallantree joins us.

"Permit me to apologize for my behavior the other day," Gallantree says. "I was impatient and rude and I'm sorry we got off on the wrong foot."

"No harm done," I say.

I look over to the bar where Sheriff Claxton continues to sit, sipping his drink. I realize he's not going to be a part of this conversation but will function as a silent symbol of Beddoe's power and influence.

"Now, sir," J.W. says, "let's see if we can sort out this confusion about what happened the other night in regards to that woman."

"Stella Garcia."

"Yes, of course. Miss Garcia."

Why do I have to keep reminding these people that she had a name?

"I know you are aware that the young lady's time of death was set by the coroner at between eight and nine in the evening, an hour at which my son Rowdy was here having late supper with me and my wife."

"I'm sure he was, Mr. Beddoe. My quarrel is not with you but with Dr. Yardley who simply made a mistake. Nothing criminal. Just human error."

He smiles jovially. "Oh, hell's bells, son, I've known Jerry Yardley for near thirty years. Man of his caliber doesn't make that kind of mistake. No, sir, what we have here is some sort of unfortunate misunderstanding."

"Well, sir, I wish it was but it's not," I say.

"This woman you met in the bar, the one who looked like Miss

Garcia—"

"It WAS Miss Garcia."

"So you say. You also say that when she left the bar she was picked up by a young man whose face you really didn't see who was driving some sort of white convertible."

"Blonde young man, white Corvette and it was Stella Garcia. She told me her name."

"And I say again, Mr. Bernardi, you are mistaken." His voice is quiet and even and without threat. "I also fail to see how or why my son could possibly be involved since he didn't even know the girl."

"He knew her, sir. They were lovers."

For the first time I see the flint in Beddoe's eyes.

"You're wrong," he says.

"Sorry, sir, it's true."

"My son is unofficially engaged to a young lady from Alpine, at present studying at a university in Switzerland. Rowdy would not be so foolish as to involve himself with a young woman from a different background than his own."

"You mean Mexican."

"If you like."

I stare at him and I realize that on this point, he is not lying. He has no idea there was anything between his son and Stella Garcia.

"Nonetheless, sir, it's true and there are plenty of people on the Austin campus who knew all about it."

"They lie."

"All of them?"

He hesitates. "Even if true, even if he dallied with this girl, we are talking about murder. No, it's ridiculous," Beddoe protests even as the first glimmer of doubt starts to show in his eyes.

"She was pregnant, Mr. Beddoe," I say quietly.

Jolted, he shakes his head.

I turn and speak loudly to Sheriff Claxton.

"Is that one of your holdbacks, Sheriff, the fact that she was pregnant, or did Dr. Yardley miss that too?"

"There was nothing in the autopsy report about pregnancy," Claxton says.

I am starting to lose it.

"Well, there sure as hell was something going on inside of Stella Garcia that begged to differ."

"You're a damned liar!" comes a shout from the open archway that leads into the room.

We all turn. Rowdy stands there, eyes wild, his complexion a pale version of scarlet. He strides into the room heading for the three of us but his eyes fixated on me.

"You're a lyin' son of a bitch!" he says, his fists clenched. Gallantree stands to try to block his way but Rowdy just pushes him aside. "Get outta my way, old man," he snarls. I get up and back off a step or two, then get ready to stand my ground.

"T.J.!" Beddoe shouts but he could have saved his breath. In an instant, Beddoe's underling has caught up with Rowdy, grabbed him tight and pinned an arm behind his back.

"Let go of me!" Rowdy shouts.

J.W. remains seated as he looks up at his son.

"Shut up, Rowdy!" he says.

"Man accuses me of murder, I got a right to—"

"You got a right to shut up, boy," he says coldly. "Don't make me tell you that again. Get the boy outta here, T.J. Toss him in a cold shower," the old man says.

T.J. starts to drag him away but Rowdy's eyes never leave mine. "You stay outta my sight, mister. I'll kill you, so help me God, I will."

I feel the hate burning into me as T.J. heads for the archway, arm around Rowdy's neck and Rowdy's arm twisted up tight behind his back. I spot Sheriff Claxton watching. His eyes are narrow slits. I see contempt in his expression and it's not directed at me.

J.W. is still standing watching the archway when he turns to me and there's a sadness in his eyes.

"My son has no manners, Mr. Bernardi. No sense of dignity. No idea at all of what he is supposed to be and how he is supposed to act. I apologize for his boorish behavior."

"Unnecessary, Mr. Beddoe," I say.

"It is to me," he says. "I thank you for coming by, Mr. Bernardi. I appreciate your forthrightness even though we disagree. I would beg of you, sir, to discontinue your public statements regarding Miss Garcia's death and any mention of my son's involvement, an allegation which I dispute."

"Mr. Beddoe—" I start to say but he puts up his hand to silence me.

"I consider myself a fair man and an honest man, sir, but when it comes to blood, those are abstract qualities. My only son has many abhorrent traits and I pray to the good God Almighty that he will grow out of them. To his mother he is a child of God without fault. Should he no longer be a part of her life, it would kill her and I will not be a party to that, no matter the circumstances. Do I make myself clear?"

"You do," I say.

"Then let us speak no more about it," he says. He puts out his hand and we shake. "Good evening, and thank you again for coming." He looks over at the other man who caught up with me at the gas station. "Jasper, show Mr. Bernardi to the door." And with that, he turns his back on me and walks over to the bar.

Marcus Gallantree moves in beside me.

"I'll walk you to your car," he says.

We go outside. It's still light out and I check my watch. It's not yet seven o'clock. Phineas will doubtless be worried about either me or the car in no particular order.

"The boy breaks his father's heart."

I look at Gallantree and realize he has just said something. He senses I was barely listening and repeats himself.

"God gave J.W. one son. With great cruelty he gave him that one."

"I won't argue," I say.

"I've known J.W. and his wife, Lillian, for over thirty years. They are decent God fearing people. How they created Rowdy I will never know but there he is and neither of them will know a minute's peace until they are dead."

"Or Rowdy is," I suggest.

"That, too," Gallantree says.

"Well, I appreciate your loyalty, Mr. Gallantree, but I'm not yet ready to confer sainthood on a man who strongarms an old and dear friend into perjuring himself in an official court document."

"The autopsy report."

"That's right," I say.

"That was my doing," Gallantree says.

"Was it?" I say, my curiosity aroused.

"J.W. knows nothing about it."

I shrug my shoulders.

"You have some friend there, counselor," I say.

"Jeremy Yardley is not my friend. He despises me."

"Oh?"

"A dozen years ago Jeremy was treating a local girl for hysteria triggered by her boyfriend's death on Omaha Beach. Turns out they'd been secretly married underage in New Mexico and she took his death to be God's punishment for what they'd done. Doc gave her an injection of the wrong medicine and she died almost instantly. He came to me immediately to represent him, sure he would be tried for manslaughter, maybe even murder. I realized right away that there was little chance of the error being discovered so I advised him to be quiet and to say nothing. I also had him write down the circumstances in case a medical board of inquiry wanted to know what happened."

"But, of course, there was no board of inquiry and that confession found its way into your safe."

"That's right. He was an excellent doctor but he was considering leaving Marfa for a bigger practice in a major city. By this time Lillian, who had always been frail, had come to rely on him much as Alexandra had come to rely on Rasputin. She and J.W. were my friends. I couldn't let him leave."

"And so Yardley stayed, hating you every minute of it."

"Yes. So you see, Mr. Bernardi, if there is blame to be placed here, put it on me, not on J.W."

"I think I'll put it on Rowdy where it belongs," I say as I open the front door of the Bentley.

"I realize you can make a lot of trouble here, Mr. Bernardi, although there is little that you can prove, especially if Sheriff Claxton doesn't dig very deeply."

"True enough," I say, sliding behind the wheel and pulling the door shut. I roll down the window.

"What're you going to do?" Gallantree asks.

"Try to get to the truth," I say, "and then expose it to the light of day. Good evening, counselor."

I spin the wheel and make a U-turn and then head back down the dirt road to civilization.

I find Phineas sitting in the hotel bar drinking an old fashioned. Two months ago he switched from martinis because his doctor told him he wasn't getting enough fruit in his diet. He's sneaking up on three hundred pounds and a rendezvous with the every disease known to man but he refuses to dial back on his eating. Unless something happens to scare the living crap out of him, he'll be dead within a decade and his loss will be tragic.

"I'd just about given you up for dead, old top," he says.

"Funny you should put it that way," I say. "How's the story?"

"Written, dictated and done with," he smiles.

"Too late for a minor rewrite?" I ask him.

He checks his watch.

"Afraid so, old top," he says. "What did I miss?"

I tell him about the pregnancy.

"Well," he says, "that certainly adds a new wrinkle to the fabric. But even without it, I expect that tomorrow morning all hell will break loose around this sleepy little burg."

I decide not to remind him that Marfa has not been sleepy for the past several weeks. At close of day, revelry breaks out everywhere. Down the street in the town square Monte Hale, the old cowboy star from Republic Pictures, entertains with the help of some of the local musicians. The bars are packed with locals and crew members trading stories and enjoying good times and good booze. Sheriff Claxton and his deputies wander around but they're not needed. Nobody gets out of line. This is Partytown U.S.A. But Phineas is right about one thing. When those hundred copies of tomorrow's L .A. Times hit the streets of Marfa, a lot is going to change.

He suggests dinner but I beg off. I'm exhausted. All I can think of is sleep. He understands and I head off to my room. As I put my key in the door I hear the phone start to ring. I go inside and cross over to the desk. I'll make this quick and then block any further calls until morning.

"Hello, this is Joe," I say.

"Hello yourself, this is Bunny."

A feeling of joy and relief washes over me. I sit down at the desk.

"Hey, how are you? Are you okay?"

"I'm fine. Why wouldn't I be?"

"I hadn't heard from you in a while and then when you called Thursday morning and got Willie—"

"Oh, Willie. Right. She sounds lovely, Joe."

"She's not lovely, she's a photographer. I mean, she works for me."

"Twenty four hours a day?"

"No. I mean, yes. I mean, she wasn't supposed to be in my room. It was a big fuck up, that's all."

"I wish you hadn't used that particular word, Joe," she says. "Not when you're talking about Willie."

"Bunny—" I whine helplessly.

"Is she pretty, Joe? Prettier than me?"

"You have this all wrong—"

"You must be very lonely, Joe. I don't blame you."

"Now stop. Listen to me—"

"I hear she wrestles alligators."

"What?"

"And she boils rattlesnakes and eats them for breakfast."

"Who told you—?"

"And not only that she once swam the English Channel towing a rowboat full of reporters."

"Bunny—!"

She starts to laugh.

"Oh, Joe, relax. I talked to Glenda Mae for almost a half hour. She told me all about Willie."

"She did?"

"She did. She sounds like a great gal to have watching your back but believe me, I don't feel threatened by her feminine wiles."

"Well, you shouldn't," I say.

"Well, I don't," she says.

"Are you sure?"

"Positive."

"Well, good and now that we have that out of the way, how are you?"

We spend the next hour talking and she sounds wonderful. Upbeat. Confident. She's been promoted, gotten a raise as well as her name on the masthead. This is the old Bunny, full of fun and ambition and with an endless love of life but also with a maturity that I had never seen before. We share memories of times gone by, the good times, and cautiously we touch on the future and what it might bring. She's not there yet but she's made it clear I'm going to be part of what's to come. For the first time she tells me where she is living and the paper she's working for and we discuss my taking a few days to visit. I tell her I'm ready whenever she is. If anything my love for her has intensified and I am sure she feels the same way. It is only a matter of time before we will be together again.

CHAPTER NINE

ome jerk is pounding on my hotel room door. Just when I finally get a decent night's sleep, erotic dreams of Bunny prancing around in my head, a lovely Saturday in Texas with no place to go and no one to see. I needn't fall out of bed at seven-thirty. I can sleep as late as ten o'clock if I choose. I am a grown man who is half owner of the company for which I toil. For now the world can soldier on without me.

The pounding continues. I roll over and look at the alarm clock which I deliberately did not set last evening. It reads 10:21. Oh. Well, in that case maybe I'd better get up and see who this unmannered cretin is. I wrap the bedspread around me and open the door, staring somewhat bleary-eyed into the face of Marfa officialdom. I think I recognize him. It's one of Claxton's deputies. The one named Boggs that I ran into in the production office a few days back.

"The Sheriff wants to talk to you," he says.

"Well, I don't want to talk to him."

I try to close the door but Boggs puts his boot in the way. "I'm authorized to throw the cuffs on you," he says.

"On what charge?"

"Inciting a riot."

"What riot?"

He smiles. One of his hands has been hidden from view as he leaned against the door jamb. Now it appears holding a copy of the Los Angeles Times. It is open and folded over to a column entitled 'A Murder in Marfa'. Beside it is Phineas' photograph.

"Oh, that riot," I say.

It takes me twenty minutes to shave, shower and dress while Boggs lounges on my sofa, scanning the newspaper's sports section. Three times he asks me where he can find Phineas Ogilvy. Three times I take the fifth. As we exit the elevator and walk through the lobby a half dozen people wave or call out to me. I see copies of the Times here and there. Everyone seems to think I've done something special. I smile in return but I am having misgivings about what Phineas, in his exuberance to win a Pulitzer Prize, may have written.

The scene repeats itself outside as we head for the deputy's squad car. A crowd has gathered. Applause breaks out. I put my hands over my head and clasp them, Joe Palooka style. On my way to possible life in prison, I play the brave martyred hero to the hilt.

Standing at his desk, I realize immediately that Claxton has no plans to martyr me and in fact he's already assured me that I am not under arrest nor will I be. But he is looking for some answers. Like Boggs, he wants to know where he can find Phineas. Rather than play games, I tell him honestly I don't know. Informing him that Phineas is staying with Vera Somebody isn't going to help him much.

"You and your friend have this town all stirred up," Claxton says.

"That was the whole idea. Now maybe you'll actually have to do your job, Sheriff."

Boggs turns on me angrily.

"You got a big mouth on you, mister," he says.

"Let it alone, Billy," Claxton says. "Take a walk and cool off."

"Maybe I better stay."

"I said, take off."

Boggs hesitates, then leaves, slamming Claxton's door on the way out. Claxton watches him go, then looks up at me.

"Billy's okay," he says. "Best deputy I ever had. He's just got a thing about Rowdy Beddoe. Thinks his old man's going to get him off again."

"Again?"

"Last year Billy pulled Rowdy in for beating up this Mexican hooker. There were no witnesses and the next day the girl changed her mind about testifying. Billy figured J.W. paid her off. Two nights later Billy was walking up to the front door of his house when three guys jumped him and threw a blanket over him. They beat the crap out of him and left him on his front stoop bleeding like a pig. Billy figured it was Rowdy and those two creeps who work for J.W. You met 'em."

"T.J. and Jasper." Claxton nods."I would have thought their loyalty would be to J.W.," I say.

"It is but J.W. won't be around forever and so whatever Rowdy wants, Rowdy gets."

"And Boggs couldn't prove it was Rowdy that jumped him."

"That's right and it's been festering under his skin every since."

The Sheriff gestures to a chair.

"Sit down," he says. He needn't ask me twice. "First thing this morning I got a visit from Nathan Pomeroy. He's the county prosecutor. He'd read the story in the L.A. paper. He wanted to know where I was. I told him everything I knew. We talked about you and your claim that the woman was alive at one in the morning. I also told him about your allegation that she was pregnant at the time of her death, most likely with Rowdy's child. We both agreed that you could be mistaken on either or both counts but could see no reason why you'd lie."

"This Pomeroy," I say. "Is he in Beddoe's back pocket?"

"No more than I am," Claxton says. "He'll bend but in the end he won't break."

"Okay," I say.

"Anyway, Pomeroy says, absent any additional evidence, given the TOD in Yardley's report, there's no way he can bring charges against Rowdy."

I nod. "So once again the snotty kid who thumbs his nose at everyone and everything gets to walk away untouched."

"At the moment, that's how it is," Claxton says. "For your information, Mr. Bernardi, as soon as I left J.W.'s last evening, I came back here and re-read the autopsy report just in case I'd missed something. I hadn't. Time of death between eight and nine o'clock. No sign of rape. No sign of sexual intercourse of any kind. No sign of pregnancy. Cause of death, manual strangulation. Signed and dated by Jeremy Yardley, M.D."

"It's a lie and I think you know it."

Ignoring me, he continues. "First thing this morning, I swung by Doc's place to have a talk with him. His car was missing. I have one of my men watching his place. When he returns home he'll be brought in."

"Do you expect to get the truth?"

"Right now, Mr. Bernardi, I don't know what is the truth and what isn't. I do know that I've got a town that is suddenly riled up because they think I'm not doing my job."

"And are you?"

"I'm trying. Under difficult circumstances."

"I know. I met him, remember?"

"I don't take orders from J.W. Beddoe," he flares angrily.

He waits for me to say something. I don't.

He reaches in his pocket and takes out a pack of Camels. He lights up and blows a huge cloud of smoke toward the ceiling.

"I do accommodate him wherever possible. It's the way things are done here."

"That's a thin line you're walking, Sheriff."

Just then there's a knock at the door and then it opens. A man enters and looks around. He's dark skinned with high cheek bones and close cropped black hair.

"Can I help you?" Claxton asks.

The newcomer checks his badge. "Sheriff Claxton?"

"That's right."

"My name is Esteban Garcia. We spoke on the telephone. I just got off the westbound train. I am here to take my daughter back to San Antonio."

Claxton rises from his chair and reaches across his desk, hand extended. "You have my deepest sympathy on the loss of your daughter, Senor Garcia." The two men shake hands. I am introduced and express my condolences but Garcia seems really not to notice me. One look into his eyes and you can't help but see it. He is a man in a fog, operating on instinct alone.

"Where will I find my Stella?" he asks.

"She's being kept at the municipal clinic but I may not be able to release her immediately."

A puzzled look crosses Garcia's face.

"On the phone you said I could come to claim the body."

"Yes," Claxton says, "and I'm sure there's no problem but I need to talk to the doctor who performed the autopsy one more time before I can release her to your care."

"I see. And where is this clinic?"

"Across town but I'm sorry, I'm shorthanded today and I can't drive you there. Let me call you a cab."

"Not necessary, Sheriff," I say. "I'll take him. Just let me use your phone for a minute." I call Skeeter and he answers right away. He says he was expecting my call. Ten minutes later he pulls into the parking lot and Mr. Garcia and I get into the backseat and Skeeter starts to drive us across town.

On the way to the clinic I learn a lot about Esteban Garcia. By profession he's a lawyer. By nature he is compassionate. He and two other men operate a small law firm in one of the poorer sections of San Antonio with a high proportion of Hispanic families. They do what they can to protect these people from the excesses of a mostly white police authority. He gets funding from a number of foundations and charitable institutions but it's certain he and his partners are not getting rich. I also learn that this laid-back soft-spoken man is ex-military and served in Europe as a Ranger before being discharged to attend college and law school on the G.I. bill. He tells me that Stella was the oldest of his five children, the youngest of which has just turned one year old. His wife Consuela has remained at home to care for the others leaving him to carry out this heart wrenching chore alone.

Skeeter pulls up in front of the clinic which is housed in a modest one story building at the far edge of town. While Skeeter waits outside, Garcia and I go inside. After a few minutes we find ourselves talking with Dr. Roger Troy, chief of staff, senior resident, morgue attendant, and key emergency room physician, all rolled into one. At age 31 and only a few months out of his internship, he and two nurses are the staff.

"Yes, the young Hispanic girl. Jane Doe," Troy says.

"Her name was Stella Garcia," Esteban says forcefully.

"Yes, sir, but we didn't know that when she was brought in."

Esteban nods. "I understand. My apologies. May I see her? I am her father."

"Well, I'm sorry, sir, but she's not here."

"Where is she?" I ask, slightly annoyed.

"We were told by Dr. Yardley to send her remains over to Trumbull & Sons. That's a funeral home on Highland Avenue, a few blocks from the hotel."

"And when did he give this order?" Esteban asks.

"Yesterday afternoon."

"Normally this is requested by the next of kin."

"Yes, but as I said, we had no idea who she was."

Esteban nods and thanks him and we exit the clinic. As I suspected, Skeeter knows exactly where this funeral home is located and within ten minutes we're pulling into their parking lot.

Oliver Trumbull is pudgy and bald, most likely in his fifties, and one of two brothers who own and operate the mortuary. The elder Trumbull is no longer involved in management having availed himself of the firm's services himself a couple of years back. True to his calling, Oliver is quiet, caring and unctuous.

"We're here about the Jane Doe that was sent here from the clinic on orders from Dr. Yardley," I say.

"Oh, yes. Miss Garcia. Dr. Troy just called. Excuse me."

We are standing in the middle of a spacious welcoming room which features four comfortable sofas and several easy chairs. There are sweet smelling flowers everywhere and soft sentimental church music is being discreetly piped in through well hidden speakers. At the far end of the room are several shelves which display miniature coffins and other paraphernalia associated with last rites and entombment. Esteban and I stand quietly and somewhat uncomfortably, looking around and, in my case, wondering where Oliver Trumbull dashed off to so quickly.

And then he returns, carrying with him a paper bag which he hands to Esteban.

"You have my deepest sympathies, Mr. Garcia."

Curious, Esteban takes the bag, looks inside and then extracts a white cardboard box. In a place marked "Name" is written 'Jane Doe'. That has been scratched out and above it has been scrawled the name "Stella Garcia." I am appalled. Esteban is in shock.

"You are a crematorium?" I say to Oliver.

"It is one of our services, yes," he says.

"And this cremation?"

"Ordered and paid for by Dr. Yardley. We were still under the impression that the young lady was unknown and indigent. I sincerely regret the misunderstanding," Trumbull says but even as he does so, Esteban is walking toward the far end of the room. We follow him. He stares up at a display of crematory urns on a shelf.

I feel sick. There will be no follow up autopsy, no way to refute the findings of Yardley's first bogus examination. The time of death will stand. There will be no definitive proof of pregnancy. Absent a motive and with an iron clad, albeit erroneous alibi, Rowdy Beddoe will not be brought to justice for Stella Garcia's murder.

Yes, I am sick and so is Esteban but for a different reason.

"I cannot bring Stella home to her mother like this." he says, almost to himself. He points a finger toward an ornate silver urn with turquoise inlays. "That one," he says.

"Quite beautiful," Trumbull says. "Sterling silver," he continues in case Esteban doesn't know what he's getting himself into.

Esteban hands him the cardboard box.

"See to it," he says.

His voice is still gentle but for the first time I see the steel in his eyes.

CHAPTER TEN

y first thought was to drive directly back to the Sheriff's headquarters and notify him of the cremation. Assuming he actually has the guts to investigate Rowdy for Stella's murder, this will come as a blow. On the other hand if he's still under J.W.'s thumb, it will come as a relief. Will the real Sam Claxton please stand up as they say on the TV show.

Skeeter points out that we'll be within a block of passing Yardley's house on the way back. Maybe the doctor has returned home. Skeeter's right. It's worth a shot. I tell him to swing by.

I don't see Yardley or his car but I do see a cruiser marked "Presidio County Sheriff" parked in the driveway. I tell Skeeter to pull in behind it. The car, a new Ford Fairlane V8, is empty but the front door of the house is open and Esteban and I are sweating as we start up the walk toward the open door. Esteban has left the urn in Skeeter's back seat.

We find Claxton in the kitchen drinking a glass of water. The interior of the house is hot and stuffy. The air conditioning is off. Claxton is feeling the heat even more than we are.

"Everything all right at the clinic, Senor Garcia?" he asks.

"No, Sheriff, it is not," Esteban says.

I tell Claxton about the cremation. His features darken. He

knows what this means to his investigation.

"We've got to find Doc Yardley," he says.

"He could be in Mexico by now," I say.

"Why would he do that?" Claxton snaps irritably.

"I don't know, Sheriff. You live here. I don't. You tell me," Esteban says. Claxton knows there's a hint of accusation in his voice but he lets it pass.

"His clothes are all here. His jewelry, such as it is. His shotgun and his hunting rifle are in the bedroom closet. He's missing and his car is missing and that's it."

"Abduction?" I ask.

"I doubt it. I've issued a bulletin for all of west Texas, eastern New Mexico and the border crossings along the Rio Grande. If he's made it into Mexico, we may never catch up with him. My big question is, why?"

"The man falsified an autopsy report." I say. "God knows what else he may have done. Maybe everything just blew up on him all at the same moment."

Claxton frowns curiously.

"You sound like a man who knows something," he says.

"Do I? Like Senor Garcia said, you're the one who lives here, Sheriff. I'm just passing through."

Skeeter drives us back to the hotel. On the way I do some thinking. Yardley is gone, why I don't know. I do know why he falsified the autopsy and I wonder if this is something I should pass along to Claxton. I'm still not totally sure about him but even if he is prepared to defy J.W. and do his job, it's going to be my word against Marcus Gallantree. Gallantree is a town father and as Claxton well knows, I'm just passing through.

We pull up at the hotel and Esteban and I get out. I tell Skeeter to stick close. I have a feeling I am going to be needing him a lot today. As Esteban and I start inside I spot the Bentley parked at curbside across the street. Phineas is up and about and I know just where I'll find him.

The hotel dining room has thinned out to the few patrons that are either having a late breakfast or enjoying an early lunch. Phineas is sitting at a table with Nick Comstock. Nick's having coffee and making notes on a steno pad at his elbow. Phineas is hovering over a platter of eggs, bacon, and sausage, alongside toast, jam and butter, orange juice and a bowl of oatmeal slathered with brown sugar. And, oh yes, a cup of coffee.

"Are you cutting back?" I ask.

"I told them to hold the home fries. Much too fattening," he says. "Now would you like to criticize my wardrobe or may I eat in peace?"

"At the risk of ruining your appetite, if you keep this up you will need a dozen pallbearers to carry your coffin and you don't have a dozen friends. Be warned."

"While you, my emaciated friend, will only need two but what happens if they are both out of town on the day of your entombment?"

I quit. I can't win. My silence delights him. He harrumphs at me and downs a huge slab of sausage. I turn my attention to Nick.

"What's up?"

He grins. "My editor got his butt reamed by the newspaper's owner so I have a free hand to write whatever I like for tomorrow's edition."

"Good," I say. "Maybe you can start by interviewing this gentleman." I introduce him to Esteban who says he will be only too happy to talk about his daughter. "Also, Nick," I continue, "you may not have heard but Dr. Yardley, the coroner, is missing under mysterious circumstances and a statewide search has been instigated to locate him."

"What's that you say?" Phineas asks, wiping his mouth with his napkin as he comes up for air.

"Excuse me, Phineas, but I was reluctant to interrupt you. Nick seems to be working while you are busy gluttonizing."

Phineas glares at me.

"That is not even close to being a word," he says.

"Excuse me, Mr. Bernardi."

There's a quiet voice at my elbow. I turn to find the balding assistant manager named Lance. He leans in close, whispering. "A moment of your time." He looks around to make sure he is not being overheard.

We move away from the table and then he whispers softly, "You received a message about fifteen minutes ago from Miss Popkin. She needs you immediately at the Hernandez house. Come alone. Tell no one where you're going."

For a moment I think it's some kind of joke, but no, Lance is totally humorless and Willie is not given to melodramatics. I hurry toward the front entrance in search of Skeeter. I hear Phineas call after me but I take Willie at her word. I tell no one.

We pull up in front of Flavia's house and I hop out of the car and jog up to the front door. Skeeter stays with the car. Before I can ring the bell, the door opens wide and Willie pulls me inside. There's fire in her eyes as she grabs me by the arm and leads me to the back of the house. I see that she has the Walther PPK tucked into her belt.

"What is it?" I say.

"Flavia," she replies.

We walk into Flavia's bedroom. She is sitting crosslegged on the bed, arms wrapped around her knees as she rocks back and forth. She is wearing a cotton bathrobe and her face is a tear-stained portrait of desolation. The door from her bedroom to the rear yard is wide open.

"What happened?" I ask.

"Rowdy Beddoe," Willie says.

I sit down on the bed next to Flavia. She continues to look straight ahead as if I am not there. I put my hand gently on her shoulder. Violently she shrugs it away.

"Tell me," I say to Willie.

"It was a few minutes past daybreak. I was still half-asleep when I heard her scream. Her folks weren't here, they'd left for the location to start preparing breakfast for the crew. I jumped out of bed as she screamed again and I grabbed my gun from the camera bag. I was down the stairs two steps at a time and when I flung open the door to her bedroom, there he was, on top of her, her nightgown pulled up and him struggling to get out of his pants. I aimed the gun at him and told him to get off her. Instead he grabbed at her and rolled off the bed with her and for a moment or so he was on the floor out of sight. And then when he stood up he had her by the throat and was using her as a shield while he edged his way toward the open doorway. I couldn't shoot. I couldn't take the chance. When he got to the door he shoved her at me and ran for it. I went over to the doorway and popped off two shots as he ran across the lawn to the next yard but I missed."

"You didn't call the Sheriff," I say.

"No. She wouldn't let me. Some of it was out of shame. Maybe a lot of it, knowing how people would look at her and maybe even feel about her. But I think mostly it was because of her father. He would have gone after Rowdy with a gun and maybe gotten himself killed. Or worse, maybe he'd kill Rowdy and spend the rest of his life in prison." She looks over at Flavia. "Poor kid. What do we do, Joe?"

"I don't know," I say.

"We can't ignore this. We can't let him get away with it. He's not going to quit."

"I know," I say, looking at Flavia. Her head is bowed. The violent shaking has subsided. She is staring at bedsheets without seeing them.

"There's only one person that can put a stop to this," I say.

Willie nods. "If he'll believe her."

"I'll tell him and he'll believe me. The question is, what'll he do about it?"

I ask Willie to stay with Flavia for the rest of the day. If possible get her to sleep and maybe get some food in her. I tell her I'll check in with her later.

"Not a word to her parents," Willie says.

"Not a word," I say.

I go out to the car and get in.

"What's going on?" Skeeter asks.

"Nothing important," I say. "Let's go."

"Where to?" he asks. I tell him. He looks at me funny. "Nothing important, huh?"

He puts the car in gear and we head on down the road.

There are two cars parked in front of J.W. Beddoe's ranch home. One's not actually a car, it's a Ford van marked "H.H. Pratt, Veterinarian". The other is a new Chevy Bel Air. There is no sign of Rowdy's white Corvette but parked next to the Bel Air is a new black and red Harley-Davidson motorcycle.

I ring the doorbell and for a minute there's no answer. I try again and then the door is opened by a pleasant looking woman, thin with a nice smile and hair just starting to turn grey. No question. This is the lady of the house.

"Yes?" she says.

"Mrs. Beddoe?"

"Yes?"

"My name is Joseph Bernardi. I'm in town with the movie company."

She continues to smile.

"Well, it is so nice to have y'all here in Marfa, Welcome, Mr. Bernardi. Won't you come in?"

That accent smacks of Louisiana, probably New Orleans, and on Lillian Beddoe, it sounds good.

"Thank you, ma'am, but I'm looking for your husband. Is he about?"

"I believe he is back in the stable with Dr. Pratt. One of our horses is doing poorly, I am sad to say. A lovely animal. I do hope we don't have to put him down."

"I hope not, too. If you could direct me—"

"Follow the path around to the side of the house. You can't miss it."

"Thank you."

"You are most welcome, sir, and if you develop a thirst which in this heat I have no doubt you will, please stop by before you leave for a nice cold glass of lemonade."

"Very nice of you, Mrs. Beddoe. I may do just that."

She steps back into the house and I start along the path that girds the main house. It is difficult to believe that this gentle woman gave birth to Rowdy Beddoe or that she had nurtured him for over twenty years. But even as I think it, I remember one of the negative tenets of Alcoholics Anonymous, the destructive role of the enabler who cannot or will not face the truth about a whiskey crippled loved one. I wonder if she realizes that she has been destroying her son with kindness all these years. I also wonder if it would have made any difference. I believe that some people are born evil to the core and I further believe that Rowdy Beddoe is one of them.

J.W. is standing next to a roan gelding in deep conversation with a slim, grey haired man in work clothes wearing wire-rimmed glasses and a floppy fishing hat. As I approach, J.W. notices me. He does not seem happy to see me and I suspect that he has read Phineas' column, maybe several times over. I would also be willing to bet that he has successfully kept it away from his wife. I stop a few yards away so as not to interrupt their conversation. He whispers something to the vet and then he walks toward me.

"I thought we had said it all the other night, Mr. Bernardi," he says coldly.

"That was the other night," I say to him looking him straight in the eye.

He searches my face and then says, "Let's get out of the sun." We walk over to a nearby oak tree which stands high and wide over a small picnic table and facing benches. He sits at the end of one. I sit opposite him on the other.

"I read the story in the out of town newspaper," he says. "Scurrilous. You cannot defend it to me."

"If I tried, you wouldn't listen, but you are not a stupid man, Mr. Beddoe. Down deep you know it is true."

"The autopsy—"

"The autopsy is a lie and we both know it. Unfortunately it is a lie which may go unchallenged." I tell him about the cremation. There will be no opportunity for a second autopsy. I tell him about the missing doctor. If he stays missing the bogus autopsy will stand. Rowdy will not be called to account.

"In any case, Mr. Beddoe, I'm not here about that," I say.

He cocks his head to one side and his visage darkens.

"Tell me," he says.

And so I tell him. The dawn break-in into Flavia Hernandez's bedroom. The attempted rape. His son's flight as Willie fired two shots at his fleeing figure. At first Beddoe had looked me in the eye but then his gaze drifted off and now I see him staring at the boundless miles beyond the ranch house. In the far distance the Chinati Mountains rise up, once home to a booming mining industry, now a graveyard for long forgotten boom towns. I don't know how big this ranch is. Maybe his property extends to the mountains and maybe even to the river beyond.

When I am finished telling him what happened this morning, he turns and looks at me once again. "I built this place for me and my wife and then after Rowdy was born, I knew I was keeping it for him, for after we were gone. I don't know why I think that. He's never cared much for ranching or for this home. To be honest, Mr. Bernardi, I have no idea what's going to happen to all this."

"Where's Rowdy, Mr. Beddoe?" I ask. "Where's your son?"

"Have you notified the Sheriff?" he asks, ignoring my question.

"No," I say.

A wry smile crosses his face.

"You, too, Mr. Bernardi?" he says. "Too bad. I thought you were better than that."

"Excuse me?" I say, puzzled.

"When someone does me a favor of great magnitude, sir, there is always a price tag involved. What's yours?"

"You have it all wrong, Mr. Beddoe. I want no favors from you and I certainly don't want your money. Only four people know the truth about this morning. Flavia wishes the incident kept secret and my photographer and I are going to respect her wishes. She is afraid that if her father finds out what happened, he will come after your boy with a gun. No good can possibly come from that."

J.W. nods in agreement.

"What do you want me to do?"

"I don't know but if he is not going to answer for Stella Garcia's death he can't stay in Marfa. Not even for one more day. The army might straighten him out. I'm sure you could arrange for the local draft board to pull his number early."

"Yes, I could do that. We could arrange it so it looked like he volunteered. That would make his mother happy."

He is hunched over, folded into himself, staring at the dry rocky ground at his feet and even now trying to find a way that will not crush his wife.

"So, I ask again, Mr. Beddoe, where is he?"

"I don't know. God's truth, Mr. Bernardi, but I will look for him and I will find him and I will do whatever has to be done. Tell that little girl, she needn't be afraid. She has my word on it."

I nod and get to my feet.

"That's good enough for me."

J.W. stands and puts out his hand.

"Thank you for coming to me first. I won't disappoint you," he says.

"I'm sure you won't," I say as we shake hands. I turn and walk away. As I pass the house I spot Lillian Beddoe at a window looking out anxiously at her husband. She is no longer smiling.

CHAPTER ELEVEN

keeter drives us back to town and we head directly for the Sheriff's station. I have no intention of telling Claxton about the attack on Flavia but I will ask him to keep an eye out for Rowdy and to notify J.W. if he's spotted. The town seems to be crowding up which is unusual since it's only a few minutes past one o'clock. I spot Steve Keller and his boys going into one of the local bars and I call out to him. He tells me that the big barbecue scene is finally in the can and rather than start somewhere new in the middle of the day, Stevens decided to wrap for the weekend to let everyone rest up.

We drive into the parking lot and Skeeter pulls up next to Claxton's cruiser just as the Sheriff is hurrying out the door. I get out of the station wagon.

"Sheriff—"

"I've got no time for you now, Mr. Bernardi." He points. "Tell it to Boggs. He's manning the desk."

"What's happened?"

"Highway Patrol just spotted Doc Yardley's car in Rudiosa," he says opening the car door.

"And Yardley?"

"I don't know."

"I'll go with you," I say, reaching for his passenger side door.

"No, you won't." Claxton says.

"Got something you need to hide, Sheriff? Why don't you want anyone with you?" I ask firmly with more apparent bravery than I really feel.

He glares at me across the roof of his cruiser.

"Yeah, maybe it's good you do come along. Get in," he growls, slipping behind the wheel and slamming his car door. I get in. In a couple of minutes we're driving out of town on Farm to Market Road 2810 heading for the low lying mountains directly in front of us. The speedometer reads 85 miles per hour.

We drive in relative silence for several minutes. My feeble attempts at starting a conversation are greeted with a tight-lipped visage and monosyllabic answers. I take in the desert scenery, such as it is, but I am unmoved. It's the same barren landscape that surrounds Marfa, hospitable only to rattlesnakes, iguanas and other anti-social reptiles.

Finally Claxton speaks.

"You want to tell me about it?" he says.

"About what?"

"Charlie Moreno. He's going on 85, kinda deaf and half blind. He lives next to the Hernandezes."

"Don't know him," I say.

"He's up early every morning. Even on Saturdays. A little before eight o'clock he hears what he thinks are two gunshots. He goes to his back window and sees a man running across his yard and out onto the street."

"Did he see who it was?"

"No, he only saw his back. Anyway he called the office. Boggs was in early so he went over there and talked to Charlie and after that he went next door and rang the Hernandez's bell. He rang it several times before your friend opened the door.

"Miss Popkin."

"The photographer."

I nod. "Willie. She's been staying in a guest bedroom."

"That's what she told Billy. He asked if there was anything wrong. She said no. He asked about the shots. She said she never heard them. When he asked about Flavia he was told she was asleep. You probably don't know this but Billy, he's got kind of a thing for Flavia and he wasn't taking any chances. He demanded to see for himself. Your friend didn't like it but she let him in. Flavia was asleep in her bed or at least that's the way it looked. Everything seemed all right so Billy left."

"I guess the old fella must have been seeing things."

Claxton glances over at me with an amused smile.

"So what did happen this morning, Mr. Bernardi?"

"How should I know?" I say.

"Did I mention that Charlie is a nosy old coot with nothing better to do than spy on the neighbors. Later this morning Skeeter Todd drove up in that beat up station wagon of his. You got out and hurried to the front door and in you went. Charlie says it didn't exactly look like a social call."

"I was there to see Willie," I say.

"No, you weren't."

"You a mind reader?"

"I'm a cop." He looks over at me. "Who was the guy running? Who fired the shots? Was anybody hurt?"

I pause before I answer.

"No one was hurt," I say.

"And?"

"That's all you need to know."

The mountains are looming much nearer now. We pass a sign that reads 'Cuesta del Burro'. I think this is the name of the mountain range but I wouldn't swear to it.

"I don't get you, Bernardi. All this, it's none of your business. You're a pencil pusher. You suck up to the newspapers and you suck up to the stars and you write a bunch of little stories about how great your pictures are and if you're good enough and the picture makes money, you get to keep your job. That about sum it up?"

"In broad strokes, sure. Close enough," I say.

"So why this compulsion to play cop? You didn't even know the girl."

"I knew her. Not for long, but I knew her. I knew her well enough to feel sorry that she'd been killed. The other thing I knew was there was no way in hell she was going to get justice in Marfa, Texas."

"I could take that personally," Claxton says, looking over at me angrily.

"Take it any way you like, Sheriff," I say, possibly as angry as he is. "She was a stranger, she was female, and she was the wrong color. When I challenged the doctor's time of death, you turned a deaf ear. When I suggested her killer might have been the son of the man who owns the town, everybody went deaf. Yeah, she had a real good chance of getting a fair shake."

"So you made it your business to find out what happened."

"Yeah, well, I'm stupid that way. It isn't the first time."

I stare out my window, seething. We're climbing into the mountains now. The road is starting to twist and turn but the Ford keeps pressing forward. We've slowed to 70 and we take some of the curves at 60.

"Sometimes stupid is good, Mr. Bernardi. I guess I'd rather a man be stupid and care than be someone who doesn't give a crap." There's a slow moving truck loaded with potatoes in front of us. Claxton whizzes by him, blowing his horn. "Chico Zapata. Nice old guy. Seven kids, all girls, and they all help him run the farm. It's quite a sight. You married, Mr. Bernardi?"

"Was," I say, "and how about calling me Joe. You're making me feel real old, Sheriff, almost as old as you."

He glances over at me and laughs.

"God forbid," he says. "So, any kids?"

I tell him no. Yvette's hard to explain.

"I've got three, just like Chico. Beth, Patty Ann, and Sylvia. Missing a few boy genes in my makeup. I love 'em to pieces but I'd rather be out helping coach Pop Warner football than watching field hockey."

"I understand," I say, not quite sure why this guy is telling me his family history.

"Look, Joe," he says, getting serious, "I know you still don't trust me. That's okay. But I want you to know that I'd love to have that snotty little kid in my gunsights, maybe worse than anybody. I truly like and admire J.W. and his wife but the boy is tearing them apart. Rowdy Beddoe is lucky I'm wearing this badge."

I look over at him. He's not talking for effect. He's dead serious.

"As for your friend Willie," he says, "she did the right thing this morning. You tell her that for me. Also tell her I'm damned sorry she missed the little bastard."

We lapse into silence. The road gets harder to traverse but then we plateau for several hundred yards and finally I can feel us gradually heading downhill. We pass a weathered sign that reads Rudiosa 10, Presidio 42, Ojinaga 43.

"Not many people left in Rudiosa these days," Claxton says. "Same for Shafter and Candelaria. Fifty, maybe sixty years ago, mining was big in these parts. Lots of people, lots of jobs. I remember Doc telling me he was born here. Said his Daddy was a foreman. But then the mines played out and folks drifted away. Doc got himself drafted and never came back, not even for a day. Said he wanted to remember it the way it was, the house, the barn, the smell of his mother's cooking, the apple orchard out back, the bluff that looked out over the river into Mexico. Those were his good times, he said.

If he never went back, in his mind, they'd never change."

"But it looks like he did go back."

Claxton's face darkens.

"So it does, Joe. So it does."

A few minutes later we spot the Highway Patrol cruiser off to our right parked in front of a ramshackle ranch house that appears to have been abandoned decades ago. Off to the right is a barn that is literally falling down. Half the roof has collapsed, the paint has worn away and the wood has turned a ghastly grey. A dark blue sedan is parked next to the cruiser.

"Doc's car," Claxton says.

As we drive in and park, the Highway Patrol officer gets out of his cruiser and walks over to us. He's young. Very young. His name tag reads "Bryce". We get out of the car and introduce ourselves.

"Any sign of him, Officer Bryce?" Claxton asks.

"Not that I can see, Sheriff. I looked in the windows as best I could. They're pretty damned dirty. I couldn't see much. I wasn't sure if I should break in so I waited for you."

"How long you been on the job?" Claxton asks.

"Be a year come October."

Claxton nods. "You did right, but there's three of us now." He pops open the trunk of his cruiser and takes out the tire iron and then walks over to the front door of the house which is boarded up. He pries at the boards and pulls them off, then wedges the tire iron into the frame and pops open the door.

We step inside. Going from bright sun to dark, we are temporarily blinded. Claxton calls out Yardley's name though there's no chance he's inside here. This house has been sealed up for many years. It is hot and musty with silty sand and cobwebs everywhere. I hear a sound off to my left near the floor and catch a glimpse of a lizard as it scurries to safety beneath a motheaten easy chair.

"He's got be around here somewhere," Claxton says. "Did you

look around outside, Bryce?"

"No, sir. I thought I ought to stay out in plain sight until you got here. What with the rattlers and the open spots where the mine shafts have collapsed, I just figured maybe it'd be dangerous walkin' around on my own."

"You figured right," Claxton says.

We step out into the sunlight and go momentarily blind as our eyes readjust to the light. I do a 360 and scan the horizon. Finally my gaze falls on an overgrown apple orchard on a rise behind the house.

"Sheriff, didn't Doc once tell you about a bluff behind the house that looks out over the river?"

His eyes travel up to the abandoned trees and then he starts to walk up a narrow dirt path that leads to the tree line. Bryce and I follow him. It's obvious this had once been a proud and productive orchard but years of neglect have turned it into something twisted and ugly. The bluff that overlooks the Rio Grande is on the other side and the three of us search for some sort of pathway. Bryce stumbles onto it and calls us over. It is badly overgrown but we are able to bully our way past long dead branches. After about twenty yards we come out into the open and as described, we find ourselves looking out over grasslands that butt up against the river. Beyond are the farmlands of Mexico.

When I look over to my left I see him. He is sitting quietly on an old wooden bench turned silvery over the years. His attention is focused on the scene below. He has not heard our approach. I tug at Claxton's shirt and point him out. Claxton nods and starts toward him.

"Doc," he says gently.

Yardley's head whips around.

"We've been worried about you," Claxton continues.

Yardley gets to his feet.

"Back off, Sam," he says. In his hand he is carrying a .38 caliber revolver which he'd been holding in his lap.

Claxton stops dead in his tracks. Bryce and I don't move. The look on Yardley's face is one of agony.

"No need for that, Doc. We're here to help you."

"No way can you do that, Sam. Not now."

"Put the gun down so we can talk. Whatever's troubling you, we can work it out."

Yardley shakes his head sadly.

"Too many years, too many lies."

Claxton moves forward a step. Yardley backs off.

"It was an accident. I didn't mean to kill that girl, Sam. It was a terrible, horrible mistake. May God forgive me."

And before any of us can move Yardley puts the gun under his chin and pulls the trigger. I jump reflexively at the sound of the shot and I stare in horror as a piece of Yardley's skull goes flying through the air in a spray of blood. And then he crumples to the ground.

Instinctively Claxton rushes to his side but he knows there's nothing to be done. He kneels there staring down at his friend's mutilated head. Then he reaches into his pocket and takes out a handkerchief and covers what's left of the doctor's face.

CHAPTER TWELVE

Claxton has radioed back to Marfa requesting the ambulance from the clinic. No doctor required. The subject is very, very dead. It took us an hour and ten minutes to get here. It'll take the ambulance the same amount of time to arrive and when we leave it will be yet another hour and ten minutes before we all arrive back in Marfa. It will still be light out but darkness will follow quickly.

The sheriff is totally confused by Yardley's 'confession'. I tell him he has it wrong. Yardley didn't kill Stella Garcia. He was referring to something else altogether. When he presses me for details, I refer him to Marcus Gallantree, the slick lawyer who had been blackmailing Yardley for years. There is no way I am getting in the middle of that can of worms.

When the ambulance arrives Dr. Troy is in the passenger seat. Word that Dr. Yardley's car had been found had spread through town quickly and then when Claxton called the clinic for an ambulance to transport a corpse, Troy suspected the worst.

"Doc Yardley?" he asks Claxton as he alights from the ambulance.

Claxton nods. "Bring the stretcher."

With our help, Troy and the driver struggle through the

overgrowth to get to the bluff. When they reach the body Troy kneels down beside it and carefully lifts the handkerchief. He blesses himself with the sign of the cross and I see his lips moving in quiet prayer. Tears have formed in his eyes. Like Claxton the doctor's death has hit hard and I become aware of just how beloved this man must have been to the people of Marfa. If there is a tragic figure in all of this, it is surely Jeremy Yardley.

It's shortly past eight o'clock when we get back to Marfa. Claxton drops me off at the hotel and goes on to the clinic with the ambulance. Troy sees no need for an autopsy. The cause of death is not only apparent but it was also witnessed. Troy says he will call Oliver Trumbull, the mortician, and have the body picked up. Trumbull will notify Yardley's wife who has spent the last couple of days visiting friends in nearby Alpine.

As soon as I walk into the lobby, I can hear the sounds of good cheer. Monte Hale is just finishing up a song to a cascade of applause. I suspect the dining room has once again become the center for camaraderie and only grudgingly available to those who wish dinner. That would be me.

When I step into the room, many sets of eyes turn in my direction expectantly and perhaps with some trepidation. No doubt they are all aware that five hours ago I left town in Sheriff Claxton's cruiser and they all want to know what's going on. Everyone seems to be here. Steve Keller and the other two 'musketeers' are off in a corner. Phineas is at a table with Willie and Nick Comstock. Nearby Rock is sharing a pitcher of beer with Chill Wills and Dennis Hopper, a newcomer who plays Rock's son, Jordy. At a table for one alone by the back wall is Esteban Garcia eating a lonely meal and if he has been cheered by the festivities he shows no sign of it. Elizabeth and James Dean seem to be elsewhere.

Tom Andre, the production manager, gets up from his table and walks over to me, speaking quietly.

"Rumors are flying," he says. "What's happening?"

I tell him as quickly and concisely as I can about Yardley's death but suggest that the crowd wait for an official statement from the sheriff. He agrees and turns to the crowd, asking for their attention. A few moments later the room falls silent.

"I know many of you are curious about the events of this afternoon and particularly the whereabouts of Doctor Yardley. Mr. Bernardi informs me that Dr. Yardley has been found and that unfortunately, he has passed away. I have no more information than that and I suggest we all wait until the sheriff is able to make a formal statement about the circumstances of the doctor's death."

A rumble of curiosity passes through the crowd but no one shouts out a question and a pall descends on the room. Slowly Monte Hale gets to his feet and with his guitar hung around his neck, he starts to sing quietly the lament of the cowboy 'all wrapped in white linen as cold as the clay'. A respectful silence fills the room as Monte sings the mournful Western ballad and when he has finished there is heartfelt but restrained applause. After a moment the quiet murmur of conversation starts to refill the room. Out of respect the atmosphere is muted.

"Hell, man, I had that nightie of hers up around her belly button and I swear to God, she was looking for it."

It's Rowdy's voice, loud and raucous and I turn to it. He has just walked into the dining room in the company of T.J. and Jasper. Everyone has heard what he said and the reaction is sharp.

"Hey, what's goin' on around here? Where's the damned party?" he says obnoxiously.

I stride over to him. I'm not a fighter but I'm ready to punch him in the face.

"Why don't you turn around and get the hell out of here," I tell him.

Rowdy laughs and I can smell the booze on his breath.

"Oh, look here. The big shot. The big mouth. Real hot to get my ass in trouble, weren't you, dago boy? You and that dyke bitch you hang around with." He arches his neck and looks past me to the table where Willie is sitting. "Yeah, I mean you, pussy cat," he calls out loudly.

I take another step toward him, fists balled, ready to swing. T.J. takes a step to block me. Out of the corner of my eye I see Rock get up from his table and start toward us.

"You back him on this, T.J.," I whisper quietly, "and I guarantee you'll be working somewhere else tomorrow morning."

T.J. looks into my eyes and then steps back.

Rock edges up next to my shoulder.

"Are we having a problem here, Joe?" he asks.

"Nothing I can't handle, Roy," I say.

He smiles when I call him Roy. I smile back. Private joke.

"Who the fuck is Roy?" Rowdy asks, swaying ever so slightly.

"Roy's the guy who's going to rearrange your face if you don't walk out of here now," Rock says.

"Oh, great, " Rowdy slurs. "First the bitch takes a couple of shots at me, then mister big time movie star says he's gonna beat me up. Well, come on, mister movie star, let's see what you got."

He weaves a little as he puts up his fists. Jasper grabs him to keep him from falling over.

"Just having a little fun with that Mex girl, that's all." Rowdy slurs. "Just a little fun. Hey, what's wrong with that? They're all the same, them Mex girls, always saying no, no, no, and what they really mean is yes, yes, yes."

He takes a step in Rock's direction and nearly falls again. I look past Rock to the back of the room. Esteban Garcia has gotten up from his table and has started making his way through the crowd.

I take a few steps to cut him off when I hear,"Rowdy!"

I turn. J.W. is standing in the doorway, his eyes cold and hard revealing the fury deep inside.

Rowdy frowns, puzzled, then smiles broadly when he sees his father.

"Hiya, Pop," he says. "I was just telling 'em all about the little Mexican girl."

"We're going home. Let's go."

"Not yet. Gonna have me a fight with this here movie star."

J.W. doesn't wait for another word. He strides over to Rowdy and grabs a handful of shirt and hair at the nape of his neck and yanks him backwards. Rowdy screams in pain.

"I told you we're leaving. Jasper, T.J., get him out of here."

The two ranch hands grab Rowdy by the arms and drag him from the room. Rowdy is alternately crying and bellowing as he is lead away. J.W. looks out over the crowd, now stunned into silence.

"My apologies to all here," he says and then he turns on his heel and strides out.

"Thanks for the assist," I say to Rock.

"We mustn't make a habit of it," he grins.

"But if needs be, we'll try," I say.

Just then Esteban Garcia tries to get by me to follow J.W. and his son into the hotel lobby. I grab hold of his elbow.

"Leave it be, Mr. Garcia. He wasn't talking about Stella."

"You think not, Mr. Bernardi. Then who?"

"Yes, who, Mr. Bernardi?"

Nick Comstock has pushed in close to me. His face is pained. "Who are we talking about? Willie won't say. Maybe you will."

"The situation's being handled, Nick,'" I tell him.

"By who? By his father? That's a joke."

"Look, I can't say anything—"

"You don't have to. Everybody here has a pretty good idea something ugly happened this morning and we can figure who was involved."

"I'd be careful what I printed," I warn him.

"Print?" he says. "A lot of good printing does. Maybe it's about time someone did something around this town instead of just talking about it." Angrily he pushes past me and disappears into the lobby.

I look at Rock and shake my head and then look past him to Willie still sitting at the table with Phineas. She raises her hands palms up in a helpless gesture.

I'm tired and need sleep. I'm also hungry and need food. I grab a passing waitress and order a cheeseburger with a side of fries to be brought to the hotel bar and when I'm sure she has it right I duck out leaving the crowd to resume its festivities as I am sure they will. I have had enough of murder and mayhem and small town intrigue. They accuse Hollywood of being Byzantine but Hollywood has nothing on Marfa.

I find a table in a darkened corner. The cocktail waitress brings me a Lone Star beer in a bottle and a dish of peanuts. I wolf down the peanuts and sip the beer which isn't Coors but close enough. Three of the out of town reporters come in and join me. I don't mind because they want to talk about the picture and not about murder. Elston Brooks works for the Ft. Worth Star-Telegram, Al Button writes for the Las Vegas Review-Journal and Paul Moran is working on a feature for Coronet Magazine. The small talk's pleasant enough until my cheeseburger arrives and then the tone turns more serious. Basically I'm a hard man to find. Willie's been great about pictures. Whatever they want, they get and the cast couldn't be more cooperative but all too often when a real problem arises I'm the man who isn't there and there's no number two to back me up. They're not speaking just for themselves but for most of the others as well. I don't argue. They are right. The out-of-town press has swelled to nineteen at last count. They need several more desks in the production office, at least two more phone lines just for reporters and better access to the mimeograph. I promise to see to it and starting tomorrow morning I will make myself far more accessible. To seal the deal I buy a round drinks. In fact I buy several. Phineas joins us and we spend a couple of hours rehashing our favorite anecdotes and revealing the secrets good and bad of the people we have had to deal with over the years. I decide that if you are going to get drunk, there are a lot worse ways than this one.

By midnight I've had enough. I sign an outrageous bar bill leaving an equally outrageous tip, bid my compatriots a good night and wander off in search of my room which, as I recall, is located on the second floor of the western end of the building. It takes me a while but I find it. I double check the room number on my key and am very pleased to see that they match. I slip the key into the lock and enter.

As I step into the room, I notice three things in quick succession. First, the light switch by the door doesn't work so the room stays dark. Second, the door leading out to my miniscule balcony is open. Odd. I have never left it open probably because I have never opened it, and the third thing I notice is the smelly burlap bag that has been tossed over my head and yanked down to my shoulders. I don't have a lot of time to think about that because something very hard crashes down on my head and I fall into a deep pool of black ink.

CHAPTER THIRTEEN

The first thing I'm aware of when I regain consciousness is that I'm in a car. Maybe a truck. I am squeezed uncomfortably between two people and the burlap bag is still pulled tight over my head. Subtly I check my hands and feet. They haven't been bound. I guess they saw no need.

I have no idea how long I have been out cold but however long, it has sobered me up. Amazing the effect fear can have on your brain and body. We are moving along a paved road. I can tell because every few seconds, a vehicle will whoosh by us coming from the other direction. I can also tell that it's raining. The spattering sound on the windshield is hard to miss and the wipers seem to be working extra hard to keep up. Now and then I hear a clap of thunder. For the past few minutes they have been moving farther and farther into the distance.

Then, abruptly, we take a right turn and the road beneath us turns rough. In fact I'm not even sure it's a road. The surface is uneven with deep ruts and the driver is constantly zigzagging as if to avoid impediments in his path. My kidneys are getting a terrible workout and my lumbar region is screaming in pain from the abuse. I fight to keep from making any noise. I have no idea what is happening but I'm sure that feigning unconsciousness is probably a good idea.

"Pull over," one of the men says.

"This ain't the place," the other one replies.

I recognize their voices. T.J. and Jasper. Rowdy Beddoe's stooges.

"I gotta whizz."

"We're almost there."

"Fuck you. I'll piss on the floorboard. Explain that to the old man."

The vehicle slows to a stop and Jasper, the one on my right, gets out. He doesn't go far. By now the rain has stopped and I can hear him doing his business.

"What the hell are we doing out here, Jasper?" T.J. asks.

"Following orders."

"From the punk? I think we're being really stupid. We're gonna get ourselves fired."

"By who? J.W.?"

"Yeah. J.W."

"Naw, he won't cross his son."

"No? Did you see him tonight? You ever see him that mad before?"

"He'll get over it. Rowdy's got him buffaloed."

"I'm not so sure," T.J. says. Then after a long pause, he says, "I think Rowdy killed that girl."

"You're crazy, T.J.," Jasper says.

"No. Rowdy's the one who's crazy. If we don't watch it, he's gonna get us sucked into something really bad."

Just then I hear the sound of an engine drawing closer. Not a car. More like a motorcycle. It gets louder and louder and then it's on top of us and stops, the engine dying.

"This isn't the place," I hear Rowdy say.

"Jasper had to take a leak. You want us to keep going?"

"It don't matter. One place is as good as another. You have any trouble? Anybody see you?"

"Nope. It went real smooth."

"Okay, get him out of there."

I hear the truck door open and rough hands grab at me and pull me across the seat and then toss me onto the wet ground. As I lay there I feel a hand reach down and yank off the burlap bag. I am looking up at a bright full moon which illuminates the scrubland for as far as the eye can see. There are also rain clouds above us and when one of them glides in front of the moon, the desert suddenly darkens into shadow. Then, just as the moon is about to reappear it is suddenly obscured as a figure moves into my sightline and I find myself staring into Rowdy Beddoe's grinning face.

"Jesus Christ!" Jasper yelps. "What did you take the bag off for? Now he's seen us."

"So what?" Rowdy says. "What's he going to do about it? Who's he going to tell?" With that he slams a boot into my side and a stab of pain courses through my body. Instinctively I try to hunch into a little ball.

"You son of a bitch, I told you I'd get you!" He kicks at me again. He catches part of my arm. More pain.

"Rowdy, you're crazy!" T.J. shouts. "Leave him alone."

"Shut up, T.J.!" Rowdy shouts back. He reaches in his pocket and takes out a switchblade knife. "Get him on his feet and hold him real tight."

"The hell I will," T.J. says. "We were supposed to bring him out here and dump him and make him walk back to town. That was the plan."

"Well, the plan has changed," Rowdy says.

"Not by me it hasn't," T.J. says.

"You mess with me, T.J., you'll be sorry. Jasper?"

He turns to the other one. Jasper's eyes are filled with fear.

"T.J.?" he whines, not knowing what to do.

"T.J. ain't gonna help you, Jasper. I ain't gonna kill this man, I'm just gonna mark him up a little bit. Now, either you're with me or against me, Jasper. Which is it?"

The pain is still fierce but there's life in my limbs and I'm trying to calculate my odds if I get a chance to run for it.

"Don't listen to him, Jasper. Come on, let's get him back to town." T. J. steps toward me and starts to lean down to help me up when Rowdy pulls a snub-nosed revolver from his jacket pocket.

"Back off," Rowdy says.

"You're not going to shoot me," T.J. says.

"No? Didn't you just say I was crazy? Hey, T.J., there's no telling what a crazy man'll do, am I right? Now this fella and me, we've been havin' it coming a while now and tonight because of him my Daddy screamed at me and took a belt to me and no man takes a belt to me without I do something about it. Now you do as I say and put this man on his feet and you hold him real tight."

"Go to hell," T.J. says as he starts to walk toward his white Ford truck. "Come on, Jasper, let's go."

I see Jasper backing away from Rowdy and then hurrying to T.J.'s side.

"Don't you walk away from me, you bastards! All the stuff you've done the past couple of years, all what my Daddy don't know about. He finds out, he'll fire your asses and you'd better believe it, I'll tell him. You'll never find work around here again, maybe not in the whole state."

Rowdy has started to walk toward them brandishing the gun. His back is to me. Still on my belly I start to edge slowly toward some scrub bushes a few feet away.

T.J. has opened the truck door. Now he stops and stares hard at Rowdy. "You do that, Rowdy, and as God is my witness, I will kill you."

"I'll kill you first!" Rowdy screams.

"No, you won't. You haven't got the guts. Maybe you can strangle young girls half your size but you haven't got the balls to face anyone your equal." As if to punctuate his point, T.J. comes around the open door and takes a step in Rowdy's direction. Rowdy quickly backs up.

"That's what I thought," T.J. says.

He climbs into the truck as Jasper gets in the other side. He starts the engine and starts to back up. Rowdy takes several steps toward the truck screaming.

"Come back, you son of a bitch! I'll get you. God damn it, I'll get you!"

Rowdy has totally forgotten me and now I half crawl, half run on all fours toward the nearby stand of scrub trying to get out of sight. If he is determined I know I haven't much of a chance against a knife and a gun. If I'm lucky I might find a large rock. David and Goliath. I'd be David, the one with the rock.

Despite the pain in my ribs, I make it to the cover of the scrub brush but it affords scant protection. I need a decent place to hunker down but I don't see one. There is a dry wash behind me, maybe four feet deep. It has collected an inch or two of water but nothing serious. He'd have trouble negotiating the motorcycle in it but there is also no place to hide. Beyond the wash I see lights. It doesn't look like a town. I'm not exactly sure what it looks like. Just lights. Red and orange and yellow, the size of soccer balls sort of floating in space and then darting this way and that without rhyme or reason. I think they represent safety but I can't be sure. Meanwhile I hear the truck roaring off in the distance.

I'm flat on my belly peering at Rowdy through the scrub. Finally he turns as if remembering me. He reacts sharply when he realizes I've gone. He starts forward a few steps, eyes scanning everywhere.

"Hey, movie man! Where'd you go? Come on out! Show your pretty face!"

The only response he gets is the howl of a coyote from far off. He cocks his head, listening intently.

'You got no place to hide, movie man. I'm gonna find you and when I do, I am gonna cut you bad. I am going to make you bleed, you son of a bitch!"

Again he lowers his head listening intently for any sign of me. The desert at night is a symphony of small sounds. The loudest are the howls of the coyotes but the prairie dogs make sounds, too, scurrying along the desert floor, brushing up against vegetation. The rats. The mice. The snakes. And now the sounds of small water droplets falling from the vegetation. All with whisper-like movements adding to the ever-so-quiet ambience.

"Where are you hiding, yellow belly? Come on out and face me like a man. You yellow, mister movie man? Huh? Yeah, I think you're yellow."

The moon is bright, lighting up everything in sight. He's been walking away from me, now he turns and starts back. If he keeps coming he'll step on me, I press down, trying to will myself to disappear deep into the sandy soil. And then a rain-laden cloud passes in front of the moon and darkness again cloaks us. At this point Rowdy makes a mistake. He walks over to his motorcycle, flipping on its headlight. He kick starts the engine and then lets it idle, pointing the light into the darkness in the direction away from me. The engine at idle isn't loud but it's enough to cover my movements and I quickly dash about thirty feet to a large boulder and duck down behind it.

Something sharp stabs at my knee and I wince in pain. I reach down and feel around. I find it and tug at it and it comes loose from the soil just as the moon reappears. I've unearthed a long handled barbecue fork, two-tined with a footlong bamboo handle. It's rusted and covered with dirt but I don't care. It's a weapon. Maybe not much of one but I'll try to make the most of it.

I peer around the edge of the boulder. Rowdy is astride the motorcycle, eyes searching everywhere. He starts to move straddling the bike, "walking" it slowly forward and swiveling the headlight. After ten or twelve yards he stops and edges off in a different direction, still moving away from me. Crawling on my belly I sidle over to the side of the wash and ease myself into it. I have one more tiny advantage. When the moon is obscured the wash is pitch black but even when the moon is high, half the wash is in shadow. I'm wearing dark clothes. I know if I flatten myself into the shadows the chances of being seen are remote. Meanwhile if I can continue on in the wash, it leads toward the dancing lights in the distance. It's my one hope. I don't have much else.

A cloud blacks out the moon. I get to my feet and run low as fast as I can, ribs rebelling with every step. I look back. Rowdy continues to swing his light back and forth in the wrong direction. Stay dark, I tell myself. Just a few seconds longer. Rowdy's figure becomes smaller and smaller in the distance. The noise of the Harley becomes more and more muted. I run, stumbling, holding my side. The cloud passes by, the moon blossoms forth and suddenly I hear the vroom-vroom of the engine and I turn. He's headed toward me now, gaining speed and I know he's seen me. He turns the wheel and sails into the air and comes down on the floor of the wash in a perfect landing. Throwing up dirt and mud and sand and rocks he races toward me. Both hands grip the handlebars, his weapons have been stashed and I realize his intention is to run me down. I keep running but he's closing the gap by the second.

At the last moment with him right on top of me, I duck to my right and in the same motion, bring up the barbecue fork and thrust it at his head. I'm not sure what I hit but I feel contact and as he flies by me, the motorcycle leans over and slams into the wall of the wash as Rowdy falls off, hitting the ground hard. The engine quits but Rowdy is still conscious, groaning in pain. I don't need an invitation. I scrabble up from the wash onto the desert floor. As I reach the top, two gunshots fill the night air. I look off toward the lights but see nothing. I look down at Rowdy. He, too, has heard the shots.

"Over here!" I shout. "Help me!"

I stagger in the direction of the shots. It's hard going but I don't look back. Rowdy's not dead but he sure looks hurt, how badly I don't know. I also don't care.

Two more shots ring out, coming slightly closer. Behind me I hear the noise of the Harley as it starts up. In a moment I see the glow of the headlight as I catch a glimpse of the motorcycle retracing its way back up the wash. Whoever is out there in the darkness, Rowdy wants no part of him. Maybe somewhere there's a way out of the wash for Rowdy and his bike. Not my problem.

Again I call out for help. No human voice responds but I do hear another shot, still closer. The sound of the Harley recedes into nothingness and I realize Rowdy has found an avenue of escape. Now, except for the rifleman, I am alone somewhere in a desert with no idea of how to find my way back to civilization. I keep moving forward, calling out every few seconds, praying to be heard. I think I see a tiny light ahead of me, different from the others.

"Hello!!!" I scream.

A voice comes back.

"Where are you?"

"Over here! In front of you!"

I hobble forward, stumbling. Twice I fall, the second time twisting my ankle. Still I get up and keep going. The light is very close now and I see it is a headlamp strapped to a man's head. I can make out a battery back attached to his belt at the hip and a .22 rifle gripped in his right hand. When I get real close, I recognize his face. James Dean.

Dean looks at me in disbelief.

"Joe?"

"What are you doing out here, Jim?" I ask.

"Shootin' jackrabbits. How about you?" he says.

"It's a long story," I say.

"Well, I'll just bet it is," Dean grins, lighting up a cigarette. "You hurt, Joe? You're walkin' kinda funny."

I tell him I could probably use a doctor. He tells me to stay put while he goes to get his car which is parked about a half-mile away. I guarantee him I am going nowhere.

It takes him twenty minutes to get us to the clinic at the edge of Marfa. His Porsche is all that he says it is and while he drives aggressively and confidently, he is not reckless. After the first minute I stop worrying. He asks me what I was doing out on the middle of the desert at this hour and I give him a shortened version.

He nods. "I never met this Rowdy fella but what I heard about him wasn't good. His old man's some kind of big mucky-muck around here?"

I smile and agree. J.W. Beddoe is some kind of mucky-muck.

The light's on and the door's open as we enter the clinic. The night nurse is at the reception desk. She takes one look at me and gets up immediately.

"I'll get the doctor," she says and heads for the rear of the clinic. It turns out Dr. Troy has a room at the back of the building where he lives, part of his arrangement with the town.

Dean sees that I'm in good hands and says he has to go. I thank him profusely for everything and he mumbles something shyly with a little wave of his hand as he goes out the door. At that moment Dr. Troy appears and he doesn't like the way I look any better than his nurse did. He pokes and jabs at me and I react appropriately. He takes me into the xray room and quickly determines that I have a couple of cracked ribs. He binds me up while the nurse cleans off my face which apparently has a bad cut and a couple of bloody scrapes. Troy checks my ankle. Twisted. No sprain. Because it's three o'clock in the morning, he suggests I sleep in one of the patient's rooms for the rest of the night and if there are no complications, I can go back to the hotel in the morning. Since I am totally washed out, I agree. What I do not agree to is one of those silly backless hospital nighties. I strip to my skivvies and slip under the sheets. My nurse is disapproving but since she is five feet eleven, weighs nearly two hundred pounds with grey hair and a nose the size of Mt. Rushmore, I really don't care.

CHAPTER FOURTEEN

I wake up to bright sunlight coming through my window. I'm achy and groggy but I know what day it is. Sunday in Marfa. The seventh day on which everybody rests, even George Stevens, though I hear it's against his religion to do so. It's also the day when a lot of the cast members, looking for respite from the familiarity of Marfa, motor down to the border to spend a few hours in the cantinas of Ojinaga across the river in Mexico. I'm told that on Sundays Ojinaga is a free-spirited festive place, happy to welcome neighbors from the north and the greenbacks they bring to the town coffers. I'd love to be one of those lucky neighbors but not today. Not in my condition. Besides, I have reports to file and scores to settle and the sooner I get to them the better.

I hear the sound of Dr. Troy's voice on the phone coming from the front of the building. He is speaking loudly and he is obviously agitated. I look at my watch. It's not yet seven o'clock. There's something going on but I'm only getting every fifth word. I gingerly slip into my trousers which are folded neatly on a chair. My ribs remain sore and painful and a sudden move sends shards of pain coursing through my body. My shirt and windbreaker are draped over the chair back. By the time I wander out to the front of the clinic, fully dressed but only partially functional, Troy is still on the phone and his voice has risen several decibels.

'Look, I'm telling you I'm not really qualified—I think you should bring someone in from the hospital in Alpine—Sheriff, I am not Dr. Yardley. I don't have the expertise. All I can do is botch things and—All right, all right, I'll be there in thirty minutes but I still think you should contact Alpine. Yes, thirty minutes." He hangs up, a troubled expression in his face.

"Trouble?" I ask him.

He looks over at me.

"That was the sheriff."

"I gathered."

"A couple of crew members working a Sunday shift found Rowdy Beddoe hanging from a wooden beam at the film location. It looks like he killed himself."

Really? I quickly compile a list in my head of all the people I know who might want to commit suicide. Rowdy is at the bottom of the list.

"The Sheriff's on his way. I said I'd meet him there," Troy says,

"I'll go with you," I say.

"Sure. Why not?" he says. "Martha!" he calls out. "Get Freddie over here. We have to drive to the movie set."

Fifteen minutes later Freddie, the ambulance driver, appears bleary eyed but awake and by eight o'clock we're driving up to the Reata facade. Because it's Sunday there was no crew call but even so, a few showed up with odds and ends to catch up on and a few others heard the news by the grapevine and appeared out of curiosity. They are standing around in little groups of twos and threes. A few curious townspeople are being held at bay on the highway by a couple of Claxton's deputies. Freddie stops the ambulance by Claxton's cruiser and we get out. Tom Andre waves to us and we hurry toward him. Willie is there alongside Steve Keller and his buddies and we exchange a look as I walk past her. She shakes her head grimly.

"This way," Andre says as he leads us to the backside of the Reata facade. Andre and his security people have been smart enough to keep everyone away from the immediate scene and as we round the corner, we find Claxton alone, hands on hips, staring upwards at the dangling body of Rowdy Beddoe. He is hanging on a stout rope from a heavy beam used as a support in the construction of the faux ranch house. He is wearing blue jeans and a black leather jacket over a tee shirt. His face is swollen and has taken on a bluish tinge and I'd say he's been hanging there at least two hours. There is an overturned keg of nails below his feet. It certainly looks like suicide but if it is, then I'm Captain Kangaroo. A narcissist like Rowdy might kill someone else but never himself.

"Guess we ought to cut him down," Claxton says.

I lean in unobtrusively to Troy and whisper in his ear. "Photos."

Troy gets it. "Maybe we should get some pictures before we do that, Sheriff. For your report."

"Yeah. Right," Claxton says and looks over at me. "I saw your girl outside. Ask her to come in."

I fetch Willie and in a minute or so, she's ripping off shots from every angle. Claxton sidles over to me.

"What the hell are you doing here, Bernardi? Playing cop again?"

"Nope," I say, "but aside from whoever killed him, I'm probably the last person to see him alive."

"Killed? Where'd you get that? Looks like suicide to me," Claxtion says.

"If you believe that, you're not as smart as I thought you were. Where's his motorcycle?"

"What?"

"Last night he was riding all over hell's half acre on that bike trying to kill me. So where is it? He sure as hell didn't walk here."

Claxton glares at me, then turns to Willie.

"Okay, that's enough." He looks over at Andre who is standing nearby. "Send in a couple of guys to cut him down."

Andre nods and in a matter of minutes two men from the construction crew appear with a stepladder and cut the rope, lowering Rowdy gently to the ground. Troy goes to the body and kneels beside it, starting his examination.

"Young lady," Troy says, waving Willie over to the body. He points to the face and neck areas and Willie clicks about a dozen shots closeup.

Claxton has been watching intently. Then he turns back to me and speaks quietly.

"Those scrapes and bruises on your face, tell me about them."

"I intend to," I say, "but I want the county prosecutor sitting in when I make my statement."

Claxton frowns.

"Nobody's accused you of anything." he says.

"And I'm going to make damned sure they don't," I tell him.

We both are distracted by the sounds of a commotion coming from the other side of the structure. A moment later J.W. appears. T.J. and Jasper are at his side. My eye catches T.J.'s. If he's surprised to see me, he doesn't show it and a moment later he looks away. J.W. goes straight to the body and looks down at it. Dr. Troy stands and steps back. For a long time the old rancher is quiet and grim faced, then he turns to the doctor.

"I'll need your ambulance to take him to Trumbull's." he says.

"Not yet," Troy says. "I need to examine the body more carefully."

"The hell you say!" J.W. shouts angrily.

Claxton moves forward.

"Now hold on, J.W. We're in the middle of an investigation here." Claxton says.

J.W. whirls on him.

"You're in the middle of nothin', Claxton. It shames me to say it but my boy killed himself. I am sick at heart. His mother will be devastated. But there is no need for any long drawn out investigation—"

"No, sir, you're wrong," Claxton says sharply. "I got a job to do and I'm going to do it. We're going to need an autopsy—"

"No!" J.W. flares. "You are not going to cut my boy up. Any damned fool can see he died of a broken neck so just leave him be."

"I'm sorry, sir, I can't—"

"And don't say 'can't' to me! If you think I'm going to let this so-called doctor slice up my son, Claxton, you better think again." He looks over at T.J. "You and Jasper get him into that ambulance."

T.J. nods and starts forward.

"Anybody that goes near that body is under arrest," Claxton says evenly. "That includes you, J.W. Doc Troy's going to take your boy back to the clinic and when he's through with him, he'll have Trumbull pick him up."

"You're making a big mistake here, Sam," J.W. says quietly.

"It won't be my first one," he replies.

They lock eyes. Finally J.W. breaks it off by looking down at his son one more time. Then he turns and strides away with T.J. and Jasper in his wake.

Claxton looks over at Dr. Troy.

"Take him back to the clinic and get me a cause of death."

"You want an autopsy?"

"Only if you know how."

"I've never done one but I know how."

"Then do it."

Claxton turns to me.

"As for you, I'll see you in my office at one o'clock. I'll have the county prosecutor there."

I nod.

"The eastbound train comes through at 11:30," I say pointedly. "I wouldn't be surprised if Esteban Garcia is on the platform getting ready to return home to San Antonio."

Now it's Claxton's turn to nod.

I show up at the Sheriff's office at two minutes to one. Claxton's cruiser is parked near the doorway next to a spanking new maroon Lincoln Continental Mark II. No doubt this means the county prosecutor is here as promised. Texas politicians know how to care for themselves.

Harrison Phelps is about what I expected. Out of shape, balding, well past middle age, affable ("Call me Harry") and a man who got his present job out of seniority rather than any special talent. The only thing missing is the cheap cigar but he makes up for it by chain-smoking Lucky Strikes. He is sitting across from Sheriff Claxton who is behind his desk. Claxton looks like a man who wishes he was already collecting retirement checks. I am also sitting across the desk, occupying an uncomfortable straight backed chair.

"So, Joe," Phelps says, "what's so damned important that I gotta be here and you can't just tell it to Sheriff Claxton."

"Well, Mr. Phelps—"

"That's Harry, son. Remember?"

"Right. Sorry, Harry. Well, here's how it is. It appears that Rowdy Beddoe committed suicide. Someone wants us to believe that but I don't believe it, Sheriff Claxton doesn't believe it and if you have ever been in Rowdy's presence for more than five minutes, you shouldn't believe it either."

"Well, since you put it that way, Joe, it does seem a little out of character," Harry Phelps says. "But what's it got to do with you?"

"Because if he was murdered, except for his killer, I am probably the last person to see him alive and under very bizarre circumstances."

"That so?"

"And if I'd gotten the chance, I would have killed him myself."

"I see."

"In self-defense, of course."

"Of course."

I proceed to tell them both about my dangerous adventure of the night before and my rescue by James Dean, small game hunter. All the while Claxton is impassive. Harry Phelps is nodding with great understanding and is certainly empathizing with my predicament. When I tell him I was taken straight to the clinic by James Dean and then treated and then put into bed and not awakened until well after Rowdy had died, he nods even more vigorously.

"All right," Phelps says with a tinge of annoyance, "subject to verification you have a rock solid alibi. What then was your purpose in dragging me down here?"

"Self preservation, Harry. Cops and prosecutors follow the path of least resistance. I was the last to see him alive, I had a motive to kill him and I am a stranger in your town. It wouldn't be the first time the authorities tried to frame me for a murder in the name of expedience, but having endured it once, I have no wish to go through it again."

Claxton glares at me.

"Marfa is not Los Angeles," he says.

"Indeed it is not," Phelps says. "We follow the law here, Mr. Bernardi. You have nothing to fear, you have my word for it."

"I'll rely on it," I say.

"Now what about these two men who abetted Rowdy Beddoe last night? Sheriff?"

"Two of J.W.'s boys. I haven't talked to them yet, but I know where to find them," Claxton says.

"And what do you say, Joe? You're well within your rights to bring a civil action against them regardless of how the Sheriff proceeds."

"My instinct says to do nothing for the moment. We might be able to use them for leverage later on."

"Indeed we might," Phelps says, standing. "Well, gentlemen, I see no reason to remain here. Our business is done with." He puts out his hand. We shake. "A pleasure to meet you, Joe. This'll all be dying down in a few days. No question. And as I said, you have nothing to worry about, Sheriff." He nods to Claxton and walks out of the office and down the corridor.

I wait until he's out of earshot before I turn to Claxton.

"What the hell did he mean by that?" I ask.

"And what would that be?"

"This'll all be dying down in a few days? What does good old Harry know that I don't?"

Claxton smiles, shaking his head. "You don't miss much."

"I try not to," I say.

"Phelps is planning a little chat with Dr. Troy to persuade him that Rowdy's death was self-inflicted. That's what J.W. wants and what J.W. wants, Harry Phelps wants. Case closed. End of story."

"And that's what Phelps meant when he said, we follow the law here?"

"Harry's sensitive about the reputation of Marfa and also Presidio County. First the murder of the Garcia woman followed by yet another murder within days. Harry wants no part of that."

"Even if it means a killer goes free?"

Claxton looks up at me levelly.

"This killer? Why not? I spent an hour with Marcus Galantree this morning. I practically had to beat it out of him but he finally told me about the secret Doc had been hiding all these years. To protect Rowdy and as a favor to J.W. he'd forced Doc to lie on the autopsy report. That, combined with what you saw, convinced me Rowdy was guilty. But you and I also know that given the phony autopsy report, there is no way Rowdy would have been brought to trial, let alone convicted. Regardless of the circumstance, Mr. Bernardi, maybe justice has been served."

"And how do you think J.W. will feel about that?" I ask.

"I don't know. For the sake of his wife, he seems to want it over and done with as quickly as possible. Suicide closes the book real fast."

"But if it turns out that Rowdy was murdered?"

"It doesn't look that way," Claxton says.

"I can think of a lot of people who wanted him dead," I say.

"So can I," Claxton responds. "Maybe that's what J.W.'s trying to avoid, dragging Rowdy's name through the mud with a murder investigation."

"Speaking of that, were you able to stop Esteban Garcia from boarding the train back to San Antonio?"

"Completely slipped my mind," he says. "No matter. Man his age I seriously doubt he'd have it in him to stage the suicide."

"Did I forget to mention that during the war, Garcia was a member of the Rangers fighting in Europe?"

Claxton looks at me in disbelief.

"Oh, shit," he mutters quietly under his breath.

CHAPTER FIFTEEN

illy Boggs gives me a ride back to the hotel. He tries to pump me subtly about what the sheriff and I were talking about with Harry Phelps, but I keep mum. How much or how little of our conversation Claxton wants to share with his deputy is his business, not mine. Since it's Sunday I have no Skeeter to drive me around so I'm going to have to improvise. I've checked Hertz once again and still no cars available. Maybe I'll just stick close to the hotel until tomorrow morning.

As soon as I walk into the hotel lobby I am accosted by a herd of reporters led by my friend Phineas Ogilvy. News of Rowdy Beddoe's death at the location has spread through town and now these nosy Nellies want the story, the whole story and nothing but the story. No longer content to be movie columnists, they are now imagining themselves as Winchell or Drew Pearson, i.e. actual journalists.

I'm torn. The axiom is, all publicity is good publicity. I'm not sure I believe that. We can get a lot of ink out of this but I don't really want 'Giant' to be known as the Texas 'murder movie'. Secondly I'm not sure how much I can really tell them given my conversation with Sheriff Claxton.

I decide to duck and dodge through an impromptu news conference. I give the surface facts without interpretation, tell them who Rowdy was and about his powerful father, J.W. Beddoe. An autopsy is being conducted but it's pretty clear Rowdy died of a broken neck at the end of a noose. No, he did not work on the crew. No, he had no connection to the movie company whatsoever. Blah, blah, blah. Most of the boys seem satisfied. Not so Phineas who knows me too well and recognizes cow manure when he smells it. After our little meeting breaks up, Phineas grabs my arm and pulls me aside.

"Now that we have sent the competition flying off in the wrong direction, perhaps you will be good enough to share with me the truth about the young man's demise. My cooperation to date has earned me that courtesy."

"You're accusing me of lying," I protest.

"My dear boy, your skills as a prevaricator are non-existent. If I could get you into a poker game for just one night, I would be able to retire for life," Phineas says.

"Off the record until further notice," I say.

"As you wish," Phineas sighs.

"It may not have been suicide."

Phineas' eyes light up like fireworks on the Fourth of July. "Murder most foul! I knew it."

"You don't know it and I don't know it, but if and when I do know it, you will be the first to have confirmation."

"I await it anxiously."

"Good. Now go find all your competitors and tell them how lucky they are to have gotten so much privileged information out of me."

"Precisely where I am headed, old top," he says as he sashays off.

Suddenly I realize how tired I am and also how sick I am of Rowdy and Claxton and the whole mess. I head for the elevators. I'll try to get a hold of Jill and maybe talk to Yvette. I might even call Bunny now that I have her number though I don't want to appear pushy. Bunny's come a long way and I don't want to scare her off. It occurs to me that I also owe a phone call to my partner, Bertha Bowles who, having read Phineas' column, must be wondering what the hell is going on here.

The elevator door opens and I find myself staring at Esteban Garcia who is just emerging.

"Senor Garcia," I say in surprise.

He nods. "Mr. Bernardi."

"I thought you were on your way back to San Antonio."

"I was," he says. "I changed my mind when I heard about young Mr. Beddoe."

"And why is that?"

"Because I am an attorney and practice among the less fortunate in my city, I am very much acquainted with violence. The young man may have killed himself or, given who he was, he might have had some help. I decided to remain to learn which."

I nod. "Not to mention the fact that your departure in advance of an investigation might be misinterpreted. Who more than you had the best reason to see him dead?"

"Who indeed, Mr. Bernardi?" Garcia says. He smiles and moves past me, heading for the lobby.

I strike out on my call to Jill. Bridget, the housekeeper, tells me that she and Yvette have gone to Malibu Pier for the afternoon. I get a similar story when I try Bunny. The only number I have is the newspaper and hardly anyone is there. When I can't cajole a home number out of the person who answered the phone, I hang up. However three is the charm.

"Hello?" I hear Bertha's voice, quiet and hesitant.

"Bertha, it's Joe," I say.

"Oh, thank God," she says with obvious relief. "I was afraid it was Jack Warner. Again."

"Again?"

"He's already called twice."

"What's wrong?" I ask.

"What's wrong? I'll tell you what's wrong. Jack Warner is wrong, that's what's wrong!" she says adamantly.

"Something I did?"

"Hell, no," she says. "Jack has spent most of the day in Anaheim snuggling up to Walt Disney. Today was opening day of Disneyland."

"The last I heard he wasn't going," I say

"Well, he went all right and now Jack wants to make a deal with us. The account of a lifetime. The ground floor on a multi-million dollar project."

"Bertha, what the hell are you talking about?"

"Jack wants to open up a Warnerland."

"What?"

"Warnerland and he wants us to handle it from top to bottom, beginning to end."

"What's he planning to do? Have Eddie Robinson wandering around among the customers shooting them with a tommy gun?"

"Christ, don't say that out loud, Joe. He's just liable to think that's a good idea."

"So what did you tell him?"

"What could I tell him? I said I'd think about it."

"Oh, God," I mutter. "Well, we can only hope he forgets all about it by morning."

"Don't count on it," she says.

"Has he said anything about what's going on here in Marfa?"

"Not a word. For the past month he's been wining and dining Lindbergh, trying to get the rights to Lindy's story."

"How about you, Bertha? Any problems?"

"Not really."

"What's that supposed to mean? Not really."

There is a long silence on the other end of the line.

"I read Phineas Ogilvy's column. Whatever is happening out there, I don't care to know. Do not send me an update. Do not write me a memo. Months from now when the picture has been released and we have been paid in full, maybe then I will let you tell me what sort of madness you were involved in."

"Thanks, Bertha," I say. "I knew I could count on you to watch my back."

"What are partners for?" she says. "I'm prepared to help out in two different ways, Joe. One, I'll stand your bail. Two, I'll get you a lawyer. Let me know if either of these eventualities pop up."

We banter like this for a few more minutes and then I hang up. The bed looks very inviting. Just an hour or two and I'll be good as new. I stand up from the desk and stretch. As I do I hear a gentle knock on my door. No, this won't do. I want no company. I want no demands upon my time. I want sleep. They knock again. Against my better judgement I go to the door and open it.

Freddie, the ambulance driver, is standing there looking very apprehensive.

"The doctor needs you at the clinic right away, Mr. Bernardi."

"Me? What for?"

"I don't know, sir. I don't ask questions. I do as I'm told." When I hesitate, he continues. "He says it's very important, sir."

I mull it over. Troy wouldn't have sent his driver like this if it wasn't urgent. I grab my jacket.

"Let's go."

The parked ambulance just outside the main entrance to the hotel has attracted quite a crowd of curiosity seekers. They become even more curious when Freddie and I appear. He gets behind the wheel. I sit up front and off we go. A woman in a monstrous Cadillac is blocking the exit as she leans out of her window to talk to a woman in a monstrous Chrysler who had been coming the other way. Freddie gives them a blast of the siren and they scatter like leaves in a windstorm. My guess is the curious are now even more curious.

Roger Troy, M.D., a newly minted doctor one year removed from his internship, is pacing in the clinic lobby when Freddie and I enter. He stops and looks at me with eyes that reflect fear and uncertainty.

"Come," he says. "In the back. Freddie, you stay here. I may need you again."

Freddie nods and sits down on a waiting room chair and picks up a three month old copy of 'Strip Mining Today'. Troy leads me quickly to the back of the building and into the clinic's small, and only, operating room. Rowdy is lying on the table his torso covered with a sheet. His head and neck are uncovered and his facial features are more grotesque than ever. Troy looks at Rowdy and then at me.

"I don't know what to do," he says.

"About what?"

"About this," He waves a hand at our corpse.

"What about him?"

"It's murder."

"You're sure?"

"Positive. I think I knew it right away when I saw the blood on his black leather motorcycle jacket."

He points to it, laying on a nearby table with the rest or Rowdy's clothes. I walk over and examine it.

"It was difficult to see in the dim light when we cut him down but I had no doubt it was there and a lot of it. That's why I was so insistent on getting the body back here. My problem is, I don't know who to tell. That prosecutor wants me to certify a suicide and I have no idea what the Sheriff actually wants. In any case I sure don't trust him. That's why I sent for you. I need guidance and you're the only one I can turn to."

He's right about the blood. There's plenty of it and because the leather jacket is such a deep black, difficult to see.

"I can't give you guidance," I say, " but I can give you advice. Tell the truth."

"That might cost me this job."

"The last doctor in this town who told a lie on an autopsy report is dead. You'd be ahead of the game. What makes you so sure it's murder?"

He points to two small puncture wounds about an inch apart in his neck. "See those wounds."

"Is that what killed him?" I ask, peering in.

"No."

"Thank God," I say.

"Why do you say that?"

"I gave him those with a barbecue fork. He was trying to run me down with his motorcycle. I just lashed out at him. I was sure I'd hit him."

"I see. Well, you cost him some blood but that wasn't the proximate cause of death. See this." He points to Rowdy's chin. I lean in to look closely. "Hairline fracture of the jaw," Troy says.

"Somebody slugged him."

"It appears that way."

"He died because someone punched him in the jaw?" I say.

"No."

I know psychiatrists who get to the point faster than this guy.

"Then what?" I ask.

He reaches over to Rowdy's head and turns it, then pushes away some matted hair. He points to a deep bloody gash in Rowdy's skull.

"That's it?" I ask.

"That's it," he says. "I'd say the head wound killed him almost instantly."

I stare down at the gash.

"That would mean that—" I hesitate. Troy finishes my thought.

"The killer strung him up dead to make it look like suicide."

"You say killer singular," I say to him. "Do you think one man could have handled everything by himself?"

"Yes, if he were strong enough and fit enough. More likely it was two people. Maybe three."

Troy is standing on the other side of the body staring down at it grimly. "I don't know whether I should be angry or insulted or both but someone must think I'm very stupid."

"How so?"

"This phony suicide was supposed to distract from the real cause of death but I promise you, Mr. Bernardi, any first year med student would not have been fooled. Someone—I'll rephrase that—the killer obviously doesn't think I'm as smart as a first year med school student. When you start looking for suspects, that might be a good place to start."

"I hate to disillusion you, Doctor, but I have no intention of looking for suspects. That's the Sheriff's job. I suggest you write up your report and your findings and take it to the Sheriff right away." When he hesitates, I add, "I'll go with you if you like."

"Thanks," Troy says. "I appreciate it. I'll be about thirty minutes."

He walks over to his desk and slips a piece paper into the typewriter.

CHAPTER SIXTEEN

Claxton reads the last paragraph of Troy's autopsy report and then lays it down in his desk.

"Okay. It's murder," he says. "I guess I'll have to do something about it." He drums his fingers nervously on his desk top. "Any thoughts, gentlemen?"

"Maybe you should start by notifying J.W.," I say.

"Right."

"While you're at it, you might want to talk to T.J. and Jasper. I heard Rowdy threaten them and T.J. in particular seemed really angry about it."

Claxton nods thoughtfully and looks over at Troy.

"No question about these findings?"

"None."

"And stringing Rowdy up, you think that was a two-man job?"

"More likely than not," Troy says. "A strong man could handle it alone but it would be difficult."

Claxton gets to his feet. "All right, no sense putting it off. Let's go see J.W.," he says.

"You don't need me," I say.

"I need you to tell him what happened out there in the desert."

I nod. He's right. Might as well get it out in the open for all the world to see.

We pile into Claxton's cruiser and it's a few minutes past six o'clock when we pull up to the parking area of J.W.'s ranch house. The Chevy Bel Air is there. So is Harry Phelps' Lincoln and Marcus Gallantree's cream colored Cadillac. The wagons are being circled.

We are greeted with wary politeness and the atmosphere doesn't get any less frosty when Claxton relays the results of the autopsy.

"You must be mistaken," Harry Phelps sputters.

"Afraid not," Troy says.

"This is unhappy news," Gallantree says, "but let's hear the whole thing, Doctor. All of it."

Troy goes through it graphically and in detail. J.W. listens stoically. All three men have been drinking. J.W. gets up from his chair and freshens his glass. Gallantree follows suit.

When Troy finishes, Phelps glowers at him.

"So what you're saying is, somebody strung up that poor boy's dead body to make it look like suicide."

"That's right," Troy says.

"Sounds farfetched to me, Doctor. I think I'd prefer the opinion of a man who's been practicin' a little longer than you have, no offense," Phelps says.

"That's enough, Harry," J.W. says.

"Now, J.W., I'm just saying—"

"I know what you're saying. Shut up. I don't take Dr. Troy for a fool. You shouldn't either." He looks up at Claxton. The three of us are still standing. "Any thoughts as to who might be responsible, Sheriff?"

"Some. I think you'd better hear what Mr. Bernardi has to say."

I clear my throat and start in. This is hard for J.W. to hear. I paint his son as a cowardly bully. Maybe he's always known it. Maybe he's always tried to shove the idea away. He can't do that any more so he just listens, grim-faced and nursing his drink. Toward the end he looks up.

"T.J. threatened my son?"

"Yes, sir," I say. "After Rowdy rode away on his bike, I never saw him again. I do know this. It was past midnight when T.J. and Jasper kidnapped me from my hotel room, probably close to one or one thirty when Rowdy showed up in the desert and I was dragged from the truck. Another half-hour before T.J. and Jasper leave and another fifteen minutes before Rowdy rides away. Dr. Troy puts the time of death at around four o'clock give or take thirty minutes. That leaves a window of one to two hours in which Rowdy was killed in the dead of night in the middle of nowhere at a time when most people are home in bed. Given all that, I would say that T. J. and Jasper need to be interrogated hard and as quickly as possible."

J.W. gets up and crosses to his desk where he picks up the phone and punches a couple of numbers on an intercom connection.

"Lou, send T.J. and Jasper up to the house, I need to speak to them." He pauses for a moment and his face darkens. "When?" he asks. He listens. "Are you sure?" Another pause. "Tell Pete not to move. I'll be right there." He hangs up and looks around at the rest of us. "They're gone," he says.

J.W. hurries from the house with the rest of us following. It's a couple of hundred yards to the bunkhouse and J.W. makes for it in a brisk stride. I find myself having to jog to keep up. The old man's physical condition belies his age. As he nears the building a man appears to greet him. I suspect this is Lou and I also suspect that Lou is the ranch foreman. He and J.W. go in. The rest of us follow.

Pete Clark is reed thin, barely twenty years old and all muscle. He's also the best roper on the ranch but to date he's never had to deal with J.W. one on one and he obviously doesn't care for it. He's sitting on a lower bunk and J.W. is sitting on a footlocker facing him.

"I d-didn't exactly see 'em leave. I n-never said that, Lou," young Clark says looking up at his foreman.

"Take it easy, son," J.W. says gently. "No one's blaming you for anything. Just tell us what you know the easiest way you know how."

"Yes, sir. Well, I guess it was maybe one-thirty. Jasper, he'd been in town and now he comes back in looking like Satan hisself was after him. The place was kinda deserted on account of it bein' Sunday and all and a lot of the fellas are gone to Ojinaga for the day. Anyway I'm layin' in my bed writin' a letter back home to my Mom and I guess he didn't see me and neither did T.J. 'cause Jasper starts yammerin' about some fella talkin' to the Sheriff and it was gonna look bad because they had roughed up this fella last night and Rowdy was with them. I didn't get the whole thing but I can tell you, with Rowdy dead, Jasper he was scared shitless and even T.J. looked real worried."

"And is that when they left?"

"They started talkin' about goin' someplace safe and about then I had to get up and go into the latrine to, uh, relieve myself which is when they saw me and all of a sudden they started talkin' in whispers and I never did hear anything else they had to say."

"And when did they leave?"

"When I came back out of the latrine, they were gone. I looked outside for T.J.'s truck. It was gone, too."

"And why didn't you report this right away, son?" J.W. asks.

"Wasn't anybody here to report it to, Mr. Beddoe. I was here by my ownself. 'Sides, I still wasn't sure what they were talkin' about."

"But when Lou returned from town, you told him."

"Yes, I did, sir. That was just a few minutes ago. The more I'd thought on it, the more I figured I had to tell somebody."

J.W. smiles and pats the young man reassuringly on his knee.

"You did right, son, and I thank you for it."

He stands and turns to Claxton.

"We'd better see to finding those boys, Sheriff."

Claxton nods in agreement.

Back at the ranch house, Claxton calls his office and talks to Billy Boggs. He tells Billy to contact the Highway Patrol, issue an all points bulletin, and then contact Diego Alvarez, the chief of police in Ojinaga, right across the Rio Grande in Mexico. They'd talked about going someplace safe. They may have been thinking about the other side of the river. As Claxton continues to give orders, I walk over to J.W.

"How's your wife holding up, Mr. Beddoe?" I ask quietly.

"Not well," he responds. "She took some sedatives and went to bed."

"I can only imagine how hard this is for her," I say.

"Yes. Hard. The truth is, Mr. Bernardi, she's been dreading this day for years. She knew it was coming. She knew it had to come. For a long time she deluded herself about Rowdy. Then for the past two years she went through the motions. She knew what he was. We both did. He was a tortured young man and there was no help for him. Now he's at peace and so are we."

He looks me in the eye and downs the rest of his drink.

A few minutes later we leave. Galantree and Phelps head for home. Claxton and Dr. Troy and I return to Marfa. Troy says he hopes the two men haven't made it across the border into Mexico. When it comes to murder charges, the Mexican government rarely honors extradition, not where the death penalty may be involved and in Texas, execution is always a possibility. We drop Troy off at the clinic and head over to Claxton's office where Billy Boggs has everything well in hand. Claxton tells Billy to go home but Billy says he'll stick around out front in case he's needed.

Just then the phone rings and Claxton picks up.

"Yeah, Diego, it's Sam. Thanks for getting back to me right away. What's going on?" He listens intently. "They are. That's good." He flashes me a thumbs up. "Where are they?" He takes out a pencil and writes something down. "El Toro Negro. Yes, I know the place. Still owned by Paco Rivera? Right." Another pause as he listens. "I guess Billy filled you in. J.W.'s son was murdered and we think T.J. and Jasper may know something about it. I want to bring them back." He listens, frowning. "Yes, I know, Diego, but the hell with Mexico City. We're talking about J.W. Beddoe's boy. J.W. can do you a lot of good, amigo, and you know it." He listens. "I don't want you to do anything. Just don't get in the way. In about an hour six men from J.W.'s spread will show up at the cantina and carry those two boys back over the border. Pretend you don't see them." Claxton laughs. "That's the idea."

Now he listens more intently. "Okay. I understand. Yes, I'll make sure there's no trouble for you. No, you have my word. Thanks, my friend."

He hangs up and looks at me. "You may have trouble on your hands."

"Trouble? What kind of trouble?"

Claxton raises his hand to stay my question as he gives the operator a number. In a moment he's connected with J.W. He tells the rancher that T.J. and Jasper are at the Black Bull, both dead drunk and showing no signs of leaving. If he'll send six men down there to bring them back, Alvarez won't try to stop them. After a few more moments Claxton hangs up.

"Well," I say, "what trouble?"

"A bunch of your actors are having a party at the Black Bull. One of them is Hudson. I don't expect any trouble but in a bar, anything can happen and the last thing you need is a bunch of your people involved in a drunken brawl."

"You're right. Can you get the owner of the cantina on the phone for me?"

"I can try." He gets the operator and places the call. It takes several minutes but then, "Paco. Sam Claxton from Marfa. Como esta?" He listens. "Good. Listen, my friend, I have someone here. His name is Joe. He needs to speak to you." Claxton hands me the phone.

I tell Rivera who I am and say I need to talk to Rock Hudson immediately. Es muy importante, I say, dragging out a smidgen of what little Spanish I know. A few moments later Rock comes on the phone.

"Joe? What's up?"

"Nothing good, Rock. Who's with you?"

"Chill and Earl Holliman."

"No one else?"

"We're the tail end of the party. What's going on?"

"'There's been a killing. J.W. Beddoe's son, Rowdy. His body was strung up on a rope at the Reata set."

"My God."

"We think the men responsible are in Ojinaga so you need to head back to Marfa right away. In about an hour there's going to be trouble that could turn ugly and none of us want to see your name or the others tied to a drunken bar fight in a Mexican cantina."

"All right. We're on our way back and Joe, thanks for the heads up."

"No problem, my friend. It's what they pay me for."

I hang up and sit back down in my chair.

"No sense your hanging around," Claxton says. "It's going to be a while."

"I'll wait," I say.

Claxton shrugs.

"Suit yourself."

We spend the next two hours in relative silence. It's twenty past nine when I hear approaching vehicles. The sun has just disappeared over the western horizon and the temperature has plummeted to fifty degrees. Claxton gets up from his desk and looks out his window, then starts toward the front of the building. I tag after him.

Several men crowd through the front door. T.J. and Jasper are in the forefront being grasped roughly by their captors.

"Put 'em in the back, boys. Separate cells," Claxton says.

"You can't do this, Sheriff. We didn't kill anybody!" T.J. says, struggling to free himself.

"The charge is assault. Mr. Bernardi will file a formal complaint in the morning," Claxton tells him.

They start to push T.J. and Jasper past me on the way back to the cell area. T.J. leans in close to me, shaking his head.

"We didn't do it," he says adamantly. "As God is my witness, we're innocent".

I watch as he and Jasper are dragged away.

CHAPTER SEVENTEEN

It's Monday morning in Marfa and all hell is breaking loose. Suddenly Hollywood is being squeezed off the front page of the local newspaper. The populace is now more intrigued by two guys named T.J. and Jasper than they are by Rock Hudson and James Dean. A real life murder has shoved make believe to the sidelines, never mind that this is actually the second murder within a week. However the first victim was a young woman of no consequence and worse yet, of Hispanic heritage. Victim number two was the lily white scion of the most powerful man in the county. Stella Garcia's demise raised hardly a ripple of interest. Rowdy Beddoe has ignited a firestorm. Those who didn't know him are saddened by his death. As for the rest of us, our reactions run the gamut from satisfaction to total disinterest. For the press, however, this is major news and they respond accordingly. Seven more reporters from seven Texas newspapers will be descending on Marfa today. Where they will sleep I have no idea nor do I care. Two light planes have already landed in the makeshift landing strip south of the town. One's from Austin, the other from San Antonio. Each represents a major television station and each is here to shoot film which they will air on their six o'clock broadcasts this evening. As if 'Giant' hadn't already done so, multiple murders have put Marfa on the map.

As for me, I am in big trouble. I am in danger of unwillingly breaking the first cardinal rule of press agentry. The story is not about the press agent, it is about the client and only the client. A press agent who allows his name to appear in print disgraces his profession and will soon be looking for some other line of work. James Dean has been blabbing all over town about our chance meeting in the desert outside of town and that, coupled with my assault complaint against T.J. and Jasper, has made me a target for every pencil pushing reporter in town. I had no sooner ordered a late breakfast in the dining room when six of them sat down at my table and began firing questions. I tried "No Comment" to no avail. I promised each of them a one-on-one interview with one of the major stars, complete with photos. I might as well have been speaking Latvian. My eggs and bacon have now turned cold. My coffee is undrinkable and my toast has deteriorated into bird feed when thankfully Phineas shows up. He grabs me by the arm, pulls me from the table and guides me toward the lobby, all the while feeding his competitors a line of nonsense about the Sheriff needing me for a lineup.

Immediately outside the front entrance, the Bentley is parked and we make a beeline for it. Phineas gets behind the wheel and I slide into the passenger seat. In back is Nick Comstock, taking notes. He looks up and smiles at me, then goes back to his notes. I glare at Phineas.

"You rescue me from that gaggle of jackals only to put me in proximity to this gentleman?"

"There are only two members of the press to whom you owe the slightest allegiance, young Mister Comstock here and myself. Keep that in mind before you make an ungrateful fool of yourself."

Phineas pulls away from the entrance and turns onto Highland Street heading toward Rte. 90. Phineas has a luncheon date with

Elizabeth in her trailer out of which will come a major profile to appear around the release date of the picture in the Sunday entertainment section. Her day is light, one scene by a stopped railway car where she and Rock alight and are greeted by a car which will take them many miles to the Reata ranch house. Phineas doesn't need anything from me but he's pretty sure I owe Nick a decent story for tomorrow's paper. Rather than argue I tell Nick what happened. When I get to the part about the dancing red and yellow and orange balloons, his eyes go wide.

"The Marfa lights. Damn. Been here four years now and never have seen them," he says.

"What are you talking about?" I ask.

"The lights. They've been around for years. Nobody knows what they are. When you go looking, there's nothing there but then a few days later, they're back, flitting around this way and that. It's bizarre."

"Well, I saw them, all right, Nick, but you're right about one thing, I sure had no idea what they were. Anyway, that's when I was rescued by James Dean." I tell him about the rifle shots and Rowdy hightailing it out of there and then Dean approaching with this light strapped to his head and the battery on his belt and the .22 in his hand. Nick can't write it down fast enough. Okay, so I'm breaking rule number one, but Phineas is right. I owe the kid and what I owe I pay in full.

We drive up toward an old-fashioned railway car which is the set for the day but then Phineas veers off and drives to the trailer area so I get to do all the walking, not him. I don't mind. I can use the exercise and if Phineas had to walk more than fifty feet at one time, it might kill him. It's a good tradeoff.

I take Nick with me up to the filming area where I promise to introduce him to Rock whom he has not yet met. On the way I ask him how he feels about Rowdy's death. Inevitable, he says.

People like Rowdy consider themselves privileged beyond all reason. Oblivious to the feelings of others they use and abuse those around them until one day they go too far. In Nick's opinion Rowdy got exactly what he deserved. Whoever killed him did the world a favor.

"Speaking of that," I say, "where were you last night, Nick, say between two and five in the morning?"

He nearly laughs in my face.

"You've got to be kidding," he says.

"Just curious," I say.

"Well, let's see," he says. "I was home alone, dead asleep until about one-thirty when I woke up from a dream. Rowdy was out in the desert doing wheelies on his Harley and shooting coyotes with his revolver. I snuck into my garage and found a stout rope which I looped over my shoulder and then still clad in my pajamas, I hopped on a tricycle to ride out to the desert with lynching on my mind—"

"Okay, okay," I laugh. "I give up. Stupid question. Sorry I asked it."

"Why? If anything had ever happened to Flavia because of him, I would have killed him. That's not a figure of speech, Joe. I mean it. "

"Does she know how you feel?"

"No, but it makes no difference. She's sold on Steve Keller and he's too nice a guy to really envy. So I pine in silence waiting for an acceptable substitute to come my way."

"And I thought you were a romantic."

"No, just a realist," he sighs.

We trudge on toward the set which, as I said, basically consists of one railway car sitting on a spur line. Nick's rejoinder to my suspicions was pretty funny so why do I feel it was a little forced and where did this little pocket of annoying gas in the pit of my stomach suddenly come from? I think maybe my imagination is working overtime.

I find Rock sitting on a folding chair beneath an umbrella reading the morning paper. I introduce Nick and we chat for a few minutes about yesterday's adventure. I warn Nick that the highly illegal kidnapping of T.J. and Jasper from Mexican soil is off the record. He understands. I leave the two of them chatting about 'Magnificent Obsession' which was Nick's mother's favorite movie. I walk over to the catering truck where Flavia and her parents are putting up the tables and chairs for the lunch break.

"What's on the menu?" I ask with a smile.

Flavia smiles back.

"Are you staying for lunch?"

I shake my head.

"Just had breakfast. How are you feeling?"

"Good," she says firmly but the smile has faded just a touch.

"Rowdy's gone now, Flavia. There's nothing more to worry about," I tell her.

"Yes, I know. I'll be fine. Don't worry about me."

"I won't," I say. "How's Steve?"

She turns back to me sharply.

"Why? What about him?"

"Nothing. I just wondered how he was. Everyone knows you and he are close."

She shoots a look toward her parents who are putting out trays and silverware.

"Not everyone," she says.

"I get it," I say.

"Those two men," she says quietly. "I understand there is no question they are guilty."

"Well, there's always a question, Flavia, but they'll get a fair trial."

"Good. That's the way it should be." She smiles at me again. "You must excuse me. I have to see to the roast." She turns and hurries toward the truck. I noticed that she got uptight when I mentioned Steve. I wonder why. I also noticed that she wasn't wearing the little black onyx fraternity pin that Steve had given her. I wonder about that, too.

I start to walk back to the trailer area where I'll find Elizabeth who may or may not be in hair or makeup. Phineas, of course, will be at her side regaling her with his endless repertoire of anecdotes for every occasion. My stomach starts to rebel again. It can't be breakfast, I didn't have any, and it isn't hunger pangs. Those I've had before. I think of Barton Keyes. Eddie Robinson played him in "Double Indemnity", the feisty insurance claims investigator who got a knot in his stomach whenever he ran across a case that smelled of fraud. I always thought it was a funny albeit fictional plot device. Now I'm not so sure. Nick Comstock and Flavia Hernandez both acting strangely and I'm developing gas. Is there something I'm missing?

I'm almost to the makeup trailer when I hear my name.

"Mr. Bernardi."

I turn to see a little old man walking toward me. Five three, grey-haired and chubby, a real life Charlie Winninger. He's wearing the ill-fitting uniform of the private security force hired by Warner's. Basically they are unarmed watchmen who supplement the local police presence.

"Do you have a minute?" he asks, looking around warily.

"Certainly," I say, groping for his name.

"Horace. Horace Plimpton."

"How can I help you, Horace?" I ask.

"I've been told you are close to the Sheriff," he says.

"I don't know about close. We've been cooperating with each other."

"I was working Saturday night. Up at Reata. The trailers were all parked a good distance away."

"Yes, I was here that day. I remember."

"I was nowhere near the ranch house facade when that boy was strung up."

"No one's accused you of anything, Horace."

"Yes, yes, I know. But you can't be everywhere at once and I stayed close to the trailers where there was a much greater chance of theft or vandalism."

"Of course, there was nothing to steal up at the ranch house."

"My point precisely," Horace says.

"And?" I'm waiting for more.

"I'm not sure I should tell the Sheriff. I'm not sure I saw it at all. I think I did, but maybe not. I don't want to make a fool of myself."

I start to get impatient. "Horace, what are you talking about?"

"I was resting in the hairdressing trailer, sitting in one of the chairs and just resting my eyes and, uh—"

"And you fell asleep."

"Yes, I believe I did," Horace says. "And then, while I was --uh—"

"Sleeping—"

"—sleeping I heard a noise like a car engine and I went to the door and I looked out and for a second or two I saw this white car down at the end of the driveway turning onto the main road."

"Truck."

"What?"

"You mean a white truck," I say.

"No, it was a car. A white car. I know the difference."

"Are you sure about that?" I ask.

"Yes, sir. The only thing is, I'd just kind of woken up and maybe I was imagining it though I don't think so, and now I'm wondering if I should tell the sheriff or just forget about it."

"What time was this?"

"About four. Maybe a little later."

I mull this over. The little knot in my stomach has turned into a clenched fist.

"All right, I'll tell the sheriff. If he needs anything else he'll let you know."

Horace thanks me and wanders off, presumably to find a spot to rest his eyes. It takes me twenty minutes to pay my respects to Elizabeth and to try to pry Phineas loose for the trip back to town. He refuses to be pried and hands me the car keys. He will hitch a ride later in the day with some crew member.

The hullaballoo hasn't abated when I drive into Marfa. Traffic clogs the major streets and the sidewalks are jammed with pedestrians. I head for the Sheriff's station and as I approach, I see a press conference in progress. Claxton is standing at the top of the stairs looking out over a couple of dozen reporters who are busy taking notes. Prosecutor Harrison Phelps is at his side. I see a couple of camera crews with TV call letters on the sides of the cameras and a couple of hefty guys holding boom mikes over Claxton's head. Willie is on hand unobtrusively taking photos of the event, why I don't know. But Willie has a motto. Keep shooting. You never know what you're going to come up with.

The conference is apparently starting to wind down as I mount the steps off to the side and then, as invisibly as possible, I slip through the door into the front room of the facility. There's no one at the reception desk but Billy Boggs is standing by a window looking out at the proceedings. He glances in my direction as I enter.

"Ignorant bastards," he says. "You'd think the Sheriff killed the guy the kind of questions they're asking."

"It's their job, Billy. Some do it well. Most don't. I have to speak to your prisoners. Any problem with that?"

He hesitates so I smile and open my jacket, raise my arms and do a little pirouette. He looks at me for a moment and then waves me to the back of the building.

"Seeing as it's you," he says with a nod.

I find them in separate cells, far apart so they can't easily communicate without shouting and being overheard. Jasper is lying on his bunk in the fetal position. He looks asleep but maybe not. T.J. is sitting on his bunk staring down at his bare feet. Claxton has taken away his shoes and shoelaces as well as his belt. They are not going to be here long. Arrangements have been made to transfer them to the Highway Patrol facility in Alpine which is better equipped to handle prisoners for an extended length of time.

T.J. looks up when he senses my presence.

"Tell me about it," I say.

"About what?"

"Everything. You're much too smart to get involved with a loon like Rowdy Beddoe."

'"The prosecutor send you in here?"

"No."

"There's a man salivating over another scalp on his belt. A two-for-one, Mr. Bernardi. Me and Jasper swing from a rope and Harry Phelps gets a big I.O.U. from J.W. Beddoe. Could life be sweeter?"

"How about if you stop feeling sorry for yourself and answer my question."

He looks me in the eye and smiles.

"Hell, why not? It started a couple of years ago. Rowdy was sniffing after this girl and her boyfriend caught him at it and beat the crap out of him. Rowdy comes to me and Jasper and offers us two hundred dollars each if we return the favor. Just enough to mess up his pretty face and maybe put him in a plaster cast." T.J. snorts, thinking about it. "For two hundred bucks I'd punch out a long-horn steer. Then a month later, the same thing happens. Different girl, different guy, different result. Guy hits his head when he falls, winds up in the hospital with brain damage. From what I hear he still can't talk right. So now Rowdy's got us by the balls because even though the guy doesn't know who we were, he can recognize us. So whatever Rowdy wants, we do. Simple as that. Steal a few dogeys from the south acreage and sell 'em over the border? Pick up a couple of thousand dollars, half for Rowdy and half for us?

Why not? Oh, it's been fun, amigo," he says bitterly, "A whole lot of fucking fun."

"And Saturday night. I mean, technically Sunday morning?" I say.

"What about it?"

"Rowdy threatens you so after you drive away, you lie in wait for him."

"No, man—"

"You chase him down, run his motorcycle off the road—"

"It wasn't like that. We went back to the ranch, into the bunk house and went to bed."

"Bullshit!"

"God's truth," T.J. says.

"Anybody who can back you up on that?"

"I don't know. The place was half empty being the weekend and all. I think they were all asleep."

"You think?"

"Well, nobody popped up out of bed and shouted 'How y'all tonight?' if that's what you mean."

"And after that?"

"We slept late. Maybe eleven. Jasper takes the truck and goes into town 'cause he needs to buy a card for his mother on account of it's her birthday comin' up and then sometime after one o'clock he comes back and he's scared. I mean crap-in-your-pants scared because Rowdy's dead and you're in talking to the sheriff and I don't need a road map to know where that's gonna get us."

"So you run."

"So we run," he says.

"After you left the desert you never saw Rowdy again."

"That's right. Straight to the bunkhouse and to bed."

"And you told this to the Sheriff?"

"No."

"Why not?"

"Our lawyer told us not to."

"Lawyer?"

"Says to us, keep your mouths shut".

"And where'd you get this lawyer?"

"From the Judge."

"The Judge appointed you a lawyer?"

"Yes, sir. On account of how we were indigent."

"This lawyer have a name?"

"Yes, sir. Name's Chaney. From right here in Marfa. Mostly does real estate."

I stare at him in disbelief and back up from the bars.

"Don't go anywhere," I say to him.

"Wasn't planning to," T.J. says.

I turn and head out to the front of the building.

By this time Claxton is back in the office and the press has scattered, searching elsewhere for copy. Claxton is furious and Billy is commiserating. He looks at me with a wry smile.

"Did you get a confession?" he asks.

"Hardly. Tell me about Chaney."

"Not my idea," Claxton says.

"A real estate lawyer?"

"Maybe he thinks it'll help him sell houses."

At that moment, the door opens and a kid walks in. A real kid. A grammar school type kid, maybe 10 years old at the most wearing ill-fitting dungarees and a tee-shirt and a pair of worn high top Keds. He looks at the three of us a little hesitantly.

"Sheriff?" he says.

Claxton smiles at him.

"Not now, Bubba. We're kinda busy."

"Yes, sir, I reckon so," Bubba says, " but I just want to tell you."

"Tell me what?"

"I just found me a motorcycle."

"What? Where?"

"In the weeds behind the Quaker Oats sign, you know the one out on 2810 at the edge of town. I was wondering, Sheriff, if someone just throwed it away, do I get to keep it?"

CHAPTER EIGHTEEN

It's there, all right. Lying on its side, just behind the huge bill-board extolling the virtues of Quaker Oats, it is red and black and shiny and spattered with blood. We have brought Willie along and she is now clicking off pictures of everything in sight. Meanwhile Claxton and I are trying our best to walk gingerly around the scene so as not to disturb any evidence. Claxton has left Billy Boggs behind to man the office in his absence.

"I'm thinking maybe we ought to bring the Staties in on this," Claxton says scratching his head.

"Fingerprints on the bike?" I suggest.

He nods. "And the blood."

"Could be that came from where I stabbed him with the fork, " I say.

"Yeah. Maybe."

The Harley is about a hundred feet in off the road, hidden in the brush. It appears that someone walked it in behind the sign to get it out of sight, at least temporarily, and Claxton's right. There could be usable prints. Slowly and carefully he retraces his steps from the bike to the road, taking in everything. He reaches the road and looks around, then starts to move slowly along the dirt shoulder still damp from the previous rain. He stops and leans down.

"Ma'am!" he calls out.

He looks over at Willie who looks back and then approaches him.

"That's Willie to you, Sheriff." she says archly.

He smiles.

"Right. Willie. I'll remember. Can you get me a shot of that, Willie?"

He points to the ground where there is a tire track left by a parked car. Because of the recent rain, the tread is sharply defined. Willie rips off a few shots as Claxton goes to his cruiser and gets on the radio to the office.

"Billy, I'm out on 2810 by the sign. Find Dave and have him bring me a bag of that plaster compound and a bucket of water— Yeah, we got a tire track. Might not mean anything or it might match T.J.'s truck. We'll see. Tell Dave to hustle. I don't want to be sitting out here all day. Also, call Lester at the garage and tell him we need a truck out here to transport the Harley back to the station and then phone the state boys and tell them we need a fingerprint guy soon as possible."

While he's talking on the radio, I'm poking around the roadside looking for anything out of the ordinary that might be a clue. Oddly enough I stumble on something. When I push some dark-stained scrub out of the way, I find myself looking at a large jagged rock jutting up out of the earth. It's big and ugly and it has the same dark stains all over it. Claxton gets off the radio and I wave him over. He bends down and takes a careful look. He stands.

"This is coming together." he says, starting to create a scenario. "Truck's parked here. Rowdy approaches. The two men flag him down. They get into an argument. One of them throws a fist at Rowdy, he falls hitting his head on that rock. Probably killed him right away. They panic. Rowdy dead this time of night after what happened out in the desert, they figure they'll be nailed for murder for sure so they invent the phony suicide." Even as he says it, he continues to look down and scour the roadside.

"I don't think it's that simple, Sheriff," I say,

"What then?" he asks.

"I don't know but it's something more," I say.

Willie joins us.

"I think I got everything, Sheriff. If you've got a camera store in town with a darkroom, I'll have prints for you sometime after supper."

"Thanks, Willie, I appreciate it," Claxton says and then he stops short, a curious look on his face, as he bends down to pick something up. Whatever it is, it's small and covered with mud. He spits on it and then rubs it against the back of his trousers and then peers at it more closely.

"What the hell is this thing?" he says. "You ever see anything like this before?" he asks, handing it to me.

I check it out. It's a heart shaped black onyx circled by baby pearls with the Greek letters Sigma Phi Epsilon embossed in gold on its face. Willie peers in and recognizes it immediately but I warn her into silence with a shake of my head.

"Strange, Sheriff. Very strange," I say.

Yes, indeed, I think to myself, there IS something more going on here.

It's pushing four o'clock by the time we get things wrapped up. Claxton has his tire cast, still wet but drying quickly. Willie is in the back of Clarence Biddle's camera store using his darkroom. Lester Browne has picked up the Harley and parked it inside his garage awaiting state forensics. And me, I'm on my way out of town for a date with an oil rig.

The work crew is busy a good distance from Reata at the site of Jett Rink's oil well derrick. Jett, played by James Dean, owns a tiny piece of Reata land due to an inheritance. Tomorrow, thanks to some clever work by the special effects crew working with the laborers, the derrick will become awash with oil as Rink's gusher comes through and James Dean becomes soaked from head to foot with oil. But that's tomorrow. Today is a day of preparation.

As I drive up, I see the two trailers that house the equipment. The rest aren't needed. The catering truck is parked nearby and a couple of tables have been put out. The work crew appears to number about a dozen and special effects maybe four or five but momentarily work has ground to a halt as the special effects people check out a set of blueprints.

I park the Bentley and head for the catering truck. That's when I spot Flavia and Steve. They seem to be arguing and are oblivious to me until I'm right in top of them. They look toward me and fall silent.

"Hi, kids," I say cheerily.

They smile back but I can tell, their hearts aren't in it.

"Not a quarrel, I hope," I say.

"Just talking," Flavia says, lying.

"That's right, " Steve says. "Nothing important." He lies, too.

"Good, good," I say, "because I'd hate to see anything happen to you two. You make a really nice couple."

"Thanks," Flavia says icily.

"I don't suppose you gave him his pin back, did you, Flavia?"

I hit a nerve and it's all over her face.

"No, of course not," she protests a little too shrilly.

"Oh? Then maybe you asked for it back, is that what happened, Steve?"

"No, don't be stupid."

"Look, breaking up isn't a sin, kids. Happens all the time."

"We're not breaking up," Steve says adamantly.

"Well, something's going on between you two. By the way, Flavia, where is that pin? I see you're not wearing it."

She throws a quick look in Steve's direction before she replies. "It's back at the house," she says.

"Oh, really," Steve says sarcastically. "Then why don't you go get it?"

"Oh, shut up!" Flavia says, quickly regretting it. "Sorry, didn't mean that."

"Sure. Okay," Steve says.

"The fact is, Mr. Bernardi," Flavia says shamefacedly, "I lost it."

"Lost it? Where? How?"

"I don't know. I can't really remember the last place I saw it. I've been pretty shook up the last few days." She looks at Steve. "I am so sorry, Steve. I feel like a fool."

"It's okay, babe. Not worth fighting over. I'll buy another one."

"No," she says, "I don't want you spending your money like that."

"Not a problem," he grins.

" But your tuition—"

"It's handled."

"It's too much money."

My head goes back and forth. It's like watching a ping pong match. Young love, ain't it grand?

"When was the last time you're sure you had it, Flavia?" I ask.

"That morning," she says. "When Rowdy— when he—" She freezes up.

"I understand. Could Rowdy have taken it?"

She shakes her head.

"I don't think so. He was coming through the open doorway when I opened my eyes. A second later he was on the bed and then Willie came in and scared him off. He never had a chance."

Steve looks at me suspiciously.

"Why all this interest in the pin, Mr. Bernardi?"

I decide to tell him because it won't be a secret long.

"It was found at the spot where Rowdy was killed before his body was moved to Reata."

Panic crosses their faces as they look at one another.

"I didn't say anything to the Sheriff but soon he's going to tie the two of you to that pin and you'd better come up with a better story than 'I lost it'."

"But it's the truth," Flavia says.

"Maybe so, but it isn't going to get you a 'Get Out Of Jail Free' card." I look at Steve. "How about it, Steve? Something you're not telling me?"

"No," he says firmly.

"Wait," Flavia says. "What time did you say Rowdy was killed that morning?"

"Somewhere around four o'clock."

"Then Steve couldn't possibly be involved, Mr. Bernardi. He was with me."

"At four in the morning?"

She nods. "Steve has his own little place over his parents' garage and I was with him there all night—"

"Flavia!"

"My folks thought I was sleeping over with a girlfriend but the truth is—"

"Flavia, knock it off," Steve says. "No one's going to believe that story."

"But I thought—"

"I know, I know and I thank you for it, but lying is just going to make it worse."

Watching them, I revise my opinion. Love is a lot grander than I thought it was.

I decide not to stay for supper. Pete and Maria grill great steaks and their burritos are incomparable but they haven't yet gotten the hang of beef stroganoff. I decide I owe both Willie and Phineas a decent dinner on my expense account and besides I am positive Phineas is wondering what's happened to his car. I am hungry but also feel mildly irritated and I'm not sure why. Maybe it's the realization that T.J. and Jasper may not be guilty after all and worse, if they are not, then who is?

I find Phineas in the hotel bar at a table with Chill Wills. I don't know what Chill is drinking but Phineas is working on Dom Perignon champagne. He, too, has an expense account. I suggest to him a decent dinner far from this madding crowd where the press will not give me indigestion between forkfuls. Chill lights up. He knows just the place. A real fine barbecue joint east of town on the road to Alpine. I didn't exactly invite Chill but on the other hand I didn't exclude him either. Like a good publicity man I invite him to come along.

Outside Phineas slips behind the wheel of the Bentley. He insists he is not too drunk to drive. I will give him a half-mile to prove it. We swing by the camera store but Willie is still working in the darkroom so it'll be just us three fun-loving bachelors off for an evening of merriment and possible indigestion.

Chill sits up front with Phineas. I stretch out as best I can in the back seat. We're about six miles out of town and Chill, a native Texan, is in the middle of a longwinded story about growing up in the tiny town of Seagoville, a few miles south of Dallas, when we hear the siren. I look out the back window and a Texas Highway Patrol cruiser is on our tail, lights flashing. Phineas glances into his rear view mirror and totally annoyed, pulls to the side of the road. The cruiser comes to a stop behind us and a very young looking officer steps out from behind the wheel. With ticket pad in hand he strides confidently to the left side of the car and looks in, ready to ask for license and registration. He sees Chill smiling up at him. He doesn't see a steering wheel. He looks past Chill to Phineas, totally confused by the right hand drive.

"License and registration, please, sir," he says to Phineas.

Phineas leans over and opens the glove compartment in front of Chill and takes out the registration which he hands to the officer. Then he digs into his wallet to retrieve his driver's license.

"May I ask the reason for this indignity, young man?" Phineas asks. "I was certainly not speeding."

"The state of Texas begs to differ, sir," the young trooper says. "67 miles per hour is a tad over the limit. "

"The speed limit is 65," Phineas fumes.

"That is correct, sir. You were exceeding the limit by two miles per hour." He scans the registration. "This car's registered to a Vera Feinblatt. I take it you're not Vera Feinblatt."

Phineas glares at him.

"Do I LOOK like a Vera Feinblatt, Officer?" Phineas asks with arched eyebrow. handing over his license.

The officer ignores him and peers at the license.

"Fine-A-Us Ogilvy, that's you?" he asks.

"That is me, more or less," Phineas says, not really bothering to correct the mispronunciation. What would be the point? "I dispute your claim that I was violating your speed laws, Officer, and I take umbrage at this unwarranted stop out here in the middle of nowhere."

"This Vera Feinblatt, she a friend of yours?"

"Most certainly not. She is an ex-wife," Phineas tells him.

The officer nods knowingly.

"And she let you borrow her car, did she?"

"She did."

The officer shrugs. "Nothing like any ex-wife I know," he says.

I'm getting hungry. How long is this chit chat going to last? I look out the back window at the Highway Patrol car, a powerful Buick painted dark blue. Phineas is right about one thing. It's a little disconcerting getting stopped by the police out in the middle of nowhere when as far as you know you've broken no law.

Phineas is getting peeved.

"Officer, I demand to know why I was stopped for such a minor infraction and if you do not come up with a reasonable explanation, other than the fact that your state seems so desperate for revenue that it is pulling over unsuspecting visitors for no reason whatsoever, we will bid you sayonara."

"Whatever the hell that means," the officer says and now HE is getting peeved. "The chief reason I pulled you over, sir, is there is a warrant out for the confiscation of this automobile and for the arrest of its driver."

"What!" Phineas explodes in high dudgeon.

"On Friday afternoon, sir, you purchased a tankful of gasoline from a filling station north of Marfa and drove away without paying for it."

"Nonsense!"

He checks his paperwork. "We got your plate number and a sort of description. 'Funny looking black English car', it says here."

"This car has classic lines," Phineas says.

"Well, that may be but these classic lines are going to have to follow me into Alpine to the station where we can fill out some paper work."

"No, we shall not. Sir, I am a law abiding respected journalist employed by the Los Angeles Times, here to cover the filming of the movie."

"That so?" the officer says, totally unimpressed. "Well, sir, you are a law abiding respected journalist whose California drivers license expired nine months ago."

"Nonsense!" Phineas says.

"Afraid not," the officer says with a faint smile.

"Officer, I can vouch for this man," I say. "I am a partner in a major Los Angeles management firm."

"That so?" Equally unimpressed. "And who vouches for you?"

I reach into my wallet and extract a hundred dollar bill which I try to hand to the officer. He raises his hands defensively.

"Whoa there, mister. That's not the kind of vouching I'm talking about. Put that back in your pocket," he says.

"It's to pay for the gas, pay for the ticket and anything left over you can donate to charity," I tell him.

Chill clears his throat.

"Let me try, boys," he says. He looks up at the young officer with a warm smile. "Son, do you know who Donald O'Connor is?"

"Sure, he's the fella makes all those movies about the talking mule."

And with that Chill tears off a vintage Francis line.

"Well, sonny boy, in the name of Texas hospitality, I think you better stop bothering these fine gentlemen and let 'em go on their way."

The trooper stares at him wide-eyed.

"Francis!" he says.

"What's the matter, son? You never talked to a mule before?"

"No, sir. I mean, I—Well, that is, it is sure a pleasure to meet you, sir."

"Well, that's fine, son, and I appreciate it so why don't you do us a big favor and take the gentleman's money to pay what's owed and let us be on our way."

"Yes, sir. I will," he says, plucking the bill from my fingers. Chill shakes the trooper's hand and autographs his ticket book. Grinning, the young man steps away from the Bentley.

"Thanks very much and you gentlemen have a nice evening."

We all watch as the officer gets back into his car and pulls by us, heading on down the road. Phineas turns and looks at Chill.

"Saved by a talking mule. I am mortified," he says.

Chill grins. "It'll be our secret, Phineas, least ways until I write my memoirs."

Phineas glares at him and then guns the car back onto the high-way. "I apologize to you both. I've gotten extremely proficient at spotting those white Sheriff's cars but this young man in black just snuck up on me."

I turn my head and look out the back window at the shoulder of the road where we and the Highway Patrol car had just been parked and suddenly it occurs to me that I know who killed Rowdy Beddoe.

CHAPTER NINETEEN

I'd like to say the dinner at the roadside barbecue joint was terrific. I'd like to say it but I can't. The mildest thing on the menu was the tabasco sauce and I ended up eating a lot of green salad. Phineas bravely tackled a rack of ribs which he seemed to enjoy until right near the end when his face started to glisten with sweat and took on a faintly chartreuse hue. Chill, by contrast, put away a T-bone, a plate of fries and two bowls of chili. Growing up in Texas has apparently provided him with a natural immunity to all varieties of Tex-Mex fare. On the positive side, we ran into no reporters.

We return to Marfa around ten and I ask Phineas to stop by the Sheriff's station. Claxton isn't there. The beefy female sergeant they all call Mama Jo is on the desk and three cruisers are out patrolling. I ask about the plaster tire cast and she says it's locked up safe and sound in the evidence closet. I also ask her what time the Sheriff shows up for work in the morning. She tells me seven o'clock. I groan inwardly, thank her and leave. I have to talk with Claxton as soon as possible but the idea of rising before seven is testing my resolve.

Phineas drops me off at the hotel. When I mention early morning breakfast to him, he turns a yellower shade of green. Chill gets out of the car with me. Since Dean is the only actor on call tomorrow, Chill says he is going to scout around the hotel for the late night poker game he is pretty sure will be in progress. Aside from performing, poker is Chill's passion and he is on a first name basis with some of the best known players from every part of the country including the legendary Benny Binion who owns the popular Binion's Horseshoe in Las Vegas. He invites me to sit in. I take one look at those come hither eyes and disarming smile and head for the safety of my room.

I'm under the covers by 10:15 but sleep eludes me. Yes, I think I know who killed Rowdy but proving it may be another matter. And there's the question of Sam Claxton and how he will respond when I tell him what I surmise. Not what I know because that would be easy. Facts are facts. A series of suppositions that lead to a probable conclusion, that is something else altogether. Maybe I should keep my thoughts to myself. Rowdy was beloved by no one except maybe his mother. Most people believe, and rightly so, that he killed Stella Garcia and also that he was likely to get away with it. Would justice be served by the arrest and imprisonment and perhaps even execution of someone who did only what the state would have done, given the chance? Sam Claxton has already implied that whoever killed Rowdy did the world a favor. As a matter of fact I remember his exact words. "Regardless of the circumstances, maybe justice has been served."

I think I fell asleep around three o'clock. Now my alarm clock tells me it is twenty past six and my eyes are wide open as the first rays of light shine through my window. I am no closer to solving my conundrum than I was last night when I drifted off. I pad my way into the bathroom, yawning. This may be a very long day.

I decide to walk to the Sheriff's station. It's about ten blocks away, twenty-five minutes on the clock with a quick stop at the bakery for a half-dozen doughnuts and two containers of coffee.

Claxton is sitting at the reception desk sifting through some paperwork when I enter. He looks up and shakes his head.

"You would think that if you had nothing to do for hours on end that you might have time to get a little paperwork in order, especially if you're a woman who, I understand, was created by God to do this kind of thing."

"I wouldn't say something like that within earshot of a woman with a gun if I were you," I say.

"If you're talking about Mama Jo Carter, that's who I'm talking about. I give her a dozen old files to update and she does half and that's it. My sister's ten year old kid could do better." He eyes my paper bag. "What's that? Breakfast?"

I take out the doughnut box and set it on his desk along with one of the coffees. "Courtesy of Bowles & Bernardi, Artists Management."

"Thanks. Mmm. Chocolate with sprinkles. Very nice." He takes a gigantic bite.

"I think I know who killed Rowdy. Want to hear?"

"Not particularly," he says. "Twelve lousy files. She says she's a high school graduate. I'm not so sure"

The phone rings. He picks up.

"Claxton...Oh, hi, Lee, good morning...." His face darkens. "What are you talking about?" Long pause. "No, that's not possible...... Because I said so......What time did you say this was?" He writes it down on a sheet of paper. "Yeah, well, I'm real sorry, Lee. I'll make sure it doesn't happen again......Yes, sir, and thank you for calling." He slams down the phone. "Damn woman."

I don't care about Mama Jo's incompetence. I want to talk about Rowdy's death. "What we have here are a series of little things, none really that glaring—"

He holds up his hand to quiet me as he dials a number.

"Morning, Mama Jo. Hope I didn't wake you." He makes a

frustrated face for my benefit. "Yeah, well, we're all tired, Mama Jo. Try to hold out for a couple more minutes. I just got a call from Lee Gustavson who says he phoned here at the office last night around three o'clock and there was no answer." His face clouds over. "Who was it that called?....What neighbor?......Uh-huh.......Did you try phoning?.......Uh-huh.....How long were you gone?......I understand but Mama Jo, you just can't leave the station unmanned....... Of course, you were worried but......"

It goes on like this for a couple more minutes before Claxton hangs up, looking perplexed.

"Well, that's just crazy," he says. "Last night around three o'clock Mama Jo gets a call from a neighbor who says he saw somebody trying to break into her house. She calls home but keeps getting a busy signal. Billy's out at the park where a couple of drunks are trying to turn over all the tables and benches. Dave's patrolling between here and Alpine and Mort is cruising north of Marfa toward Fort Davis. She's got an invalid mother at home so she locks up and leaves. When she gets to her house, everything's quiet, the doors are all locked and her mother is sound asleep in her bed."

"And the phone?"

"That's the screwy thing. The phone line at the side of the house had been cut."

"And how long was Mama Jo out of the office?"

"She says no more than thirty minutes."

I nod. Thirty minutes. More than enough time.

"I think you'd better check your evidence closet," I say.

"What for?"

"Maybe what's left of the plaster cast of the tire tread, If anything."

"I've got the only key," Claxton says.

"Humor me," I say.

Claxton checks out his key ring and selects one of them as we walk toward the rear of the building. Even before we get to the door, we can see that the padlock has been smashed and the hasp pried open. Claxton pushes open the door and flips on the light switch. We both react to what we see. The tiny little room has been vandalized. Everything has been pulled from the shelves and the cast of tire tread lies shattered on the floor, a mass of unusable pieces of plaster.

"Son of a bitch," Claxton mutters softly under his breath. He looks at me. "What do you know about this?" he asks.

"Know? Nothing. But I can guess," I say.

"Tell me."

"You won't be happy, Sheriff."

"Spit it out."

"Billy Boggs," I say.

He screws up his face in an expression of total disbelief. I might as well have said Kris Kringle.

"You're crazy," he says as he flips off the light and walks out of the room. I shut the door and follow him back to his office.

"Check the back door. See if it was forced," I say.

"You check it," he says angrily as he sits down at his desk.

So I do. In a moment or two I'm back.

"Still locked. No sign of forced entry. Your intruder had a key."

"I know the boy. He's no killer," Claxton says.

"He was on duty Sunday morning."

"He might have been."

"You know he was."

I sit down in the chair next to his desk.

"I didn't invite you to sit down," he says.

I stay seated.

"Aren't you the one that told me Billy hated Rowdy?"

"Hate's not murder," he says.

"No, it's not," I say. "At around four o'clock the security guard saw a white car leaving the movie set."

"What's your point?"

"Your cruisers are white."

"White and pale green," Claxton says.

"At a distance pale green looks like white."

"Maybe to you."

"That fraternity pin you found at the murder site. Billy had stolen it from Flavia's room."

"Bullshit."

"He's the only one who could have."

"This is crap, Bernardi. Get out of here."

"It's early Sunday morning. Boggs is on patrol. He spots Rowdy on his motorcycle. He's riding erratically. Maybe he's drunk. He pulls him over to the side of the road. Rowdy's lost blood due to the stab wounds in his throat but Boggs doesn't know that. He's sure Rowdy's been drinking. Rowdy gets belligerent. Maybe he throws a punch. Boggs throws one back and Rowdy goes down, hits the back of his head on that jagged rock and dies instantly."

"This is what you Hollywood people do, make things up and think people will believe 'em?"

"Some people will."

"Even if you're right," Claxton says, "that's an accident, not murder."

"You're right but Boggs panics. He didn't mean to do it but everybody knows he hated Rowdy. Who's going to believe him? They'll find the body and the bike and all of a sudden he's got to answer questions he can't answer. Which is when he dreams up the idea of faking the suicide. He hides the bike behind the sign, drives Rowdy's body to the ranch house facade and strings it up."

"No, you make no sense."

"Are you deliberately being obtuse, Sheriff? You're the one who told me Billy went into Flavia's bedroom to make sure she was okay. The pin was there when he walked in, it was gone when he walked out. Could have been anger. More likely it was jealousy. For God's sake, Sheriff, open your mind. I'm giving you a chance to do something about this before you read about it in tomorrow's paper and I guarantee it will be in tomorrow's paper if you keep stonewalling."

He stares across the desk at me. I'm beginning to understand that Billy is the son that Claxton never had and my accusation is killing him. I meet his look. The fight has gone out of him.

"It makes no difference how much you may like Billy personally or how much you may have despised Rowdy Beddoe, the issue is murder and you are the Sheriff."

For a long time he remains silent. "I have no proof," he says quietly.

"You had proof with that plaster tire cast but Boggs destroyed it.'"

Claxton frowns and looks away.

"Maybe we can still get some proof," I say. "I have an idea. It might work. We need to go back to the scene of the murder."

"All right, we'll do it your way," he says without enthusiasm. "Pablo Moreno's on patrol. I'll bring him in to cover the desk."

I nod.

"What's the plan?" he asks.

"We're going to need some water," I say.

CHAPTER TWENTY

Claxton pulls up to the side of the road well short of the Quaker Oats billboard. We get out and I retrieve the jug of water from the trunk. We walk forward to the spot where we made the first plaster cast. It's been pretty much obliterated by the first attempt and by the natural effects of the weather since then. Claxton stares down at the spot and shakes us head.

"This isn't going to work. Billy's not stupid," he says.

"We'll see," I say as I start sprinkling water on the remnants of the former tread mark. Not a lot. Just enough to dampen the ground so it'll hold the tread design. After about a minute, I back away.

"I think that'll do it."

"Your show," Claxton says laconically as he walks back to his cruiser. He starts the engine and pulls forward slowly. I guide him to the damp spot and he rolls over it with his front left tire, then backs up and stops. I look down, pleased, and give him a thumbs up. The tread is sharply defined.

"Okay, Sheriff, give him a holler," I say.

Claxton nods. "I still think you're nuts."

He backs the cruiser up to its former spot and I see him reach for the radio mike. The plan is simple and even if it works, it's not the sort of proof you can bring into a court of law. However, it might be enough to convince Claxton that I'm right about Boggs. Boggs will bring a bucket of water and another sack of plaster here to the site. Claxton will tell him to make another cast to replace the one that was destroyed. If Boggs does what he's told and does it well I may be wrong about him. But if, as I suspect, he botches the job, then I'll know I'm right. There are a lot of ways Boggs can sabotage the making of the cast, the most likely being to make the mixture too watery. It will not only not harden into a usable cast but it will wash away the sharp edges of the tread design rendering it useless for a second attempt.

Claxton gets out of the cruiser and walks up to me.

"All set?" I ask.

"He's on his way," Claxton says. He shakes his head as he looks at the tread. "I'm trying to keep an open mind, but I don't buy this, Joe. Not for a second. We've got our killers locked up in Alpine. Only reason I'm going along is so I don't have to read some half-baked story in tomorrow's paper."

He wanders off, heading toward the billboard, eyes peering closely at the ground as if hoping against hope that he will find some new clue that will exonerate Boggs and lock up the case against TJ. and Jasper. It's another hot day with a cloudless sky and I am starting to sweat. This is not how I envisioned spending my days in Marfa and I just want this whole mess to be over with. I look down the road toward town for any sign of Boggs' approaching cruiser. The road is empty as it has been since we got here. This road over the mountains to the ghost towns of days gone by is mostly deserted.

"Joe!"

I hear Claxton calling to me from the other side of the billboard.

"I think I've found something," he calls out.

I hurry into the scrub and make my way to the spot where the motorcycle had been abandoned. Claxton is waiting for me.

"What is it? What did you find?" I ask.

He ignores my question,

"Let's suppose you're right, Joe. Do you think justice will really be served by putting Billy on trial?"

"No, probably not," I say, "but that's not my decision to make. Or yours, either, Sheriff."

"We could make it our decision," he says, keeping his eyes focused on mine. I don't like what he's said or the way he's said it.

"I don't think so," I say. "Let's say Rowdy was killed by accident or maybe in self-defense. It'll be up to Harry Phelps to prosecute or not prosecute."

"He's beholden to J.W. Beddoe. What do you think he'll do?"

"I don't know," I say.

Claxton snorts. He's not amused.

"You know better than that, Joe." He hesitates for a moment. "You have it wrong, you know. Not all of it, but most of it," Claxton says. I see his hand rest lazily on the butt of his holstered service revolver and suddenly, despite the heat, I feel a chill settle into my shoulder blades.

"Billy didn't string up Rowdy's body, I did," Claxton says

I look for some sign that he's lying. I don't see any. Still I say, "I don't believe you."

"Billy was on a patrol when he spotted Rowdy on his motorcycle weaving all over the road. He pulled him over to the shoulder and ordered him off his bike. Rowdy mumbled something Billy couldn't hear. Rowdy wouldn't move so Billy grabbed him and pulled him off the bike. And you were right. Rowdy took a swing at him and Billy went down. Maybe that's when that funny looking little pin fell out of Billy's pocket. Anyway, Billy got up and swung back, hitting him on the jaw. Rowdy fell and he didn't move. Billy knelt down beside him and knew right away he was dead. He was scared, Joe. Terrified. He went to find a phone booth and called me at home. I told him to sit tight. When I got here thirty minutes later, Billy was sitting behind the wheel of his car, his head in his hands. He'd been crying. Rowdy was still lying where he fell. The motorcycle was still overturned on the shoulder."

"Okay, it was an accident."

"But you said it yourself, Joe. Considering all the bad blood between them, who was going to believe Billy's story?"

"So everything else that happened, that was your doing."

"I told Billy to go home and not worry, that I'd take care of things. He didn't want me to. He's a good kid with a conscience. I warned him that his conscience was going to get him sent to prison for a lot of years unless he ignored it."

"So you ditched the motorcycle, drove Rowdy to the location site, and hung his body. It was you that the watchman saw leaving, not Billy."

"That's right."

"And the tire track?"

"Could have been either of us. Doesn't make any difference, not now," Claxton says.

I look into his eyes and I see the truth.

"Billy's not coming, is he?"

"No, he's not, Joe."

"That leaves just you and me," I say.

"That's right. I don't want to hurt you, Joe, but I'm in deep and things are falling apart."

"Who was it said, life's what happens when God has other plans for you?"

"I have a wife and three girls. They need me. They're worth more to me than a dozen Rowdy Beddoes or a Billy Boggs or even you, Joe."

"That doesn't sound good for my side."

"Give me your word that you'll forget everything we've just talked about and we can both walk out of here."

"I can hardly believe you mean that, Sheriff?"

"But I do. Nothing happened to Rowdy last Sunday that wouldn't have happened if the law had been allowed to operate properly. He'd have been strung up by the state of Texas, not me, and the result would have been the same. Justice for Stella Garcia. Show me where I'm wrong."

"In principle I can't."

"And?"

"I could promise you anything right now to save my hide but it would be a promise I couldn't keep. Not with T.J. and Jasper facing trial for a murder they didn't commit."

Claxton nods.

"I'm aware of that but whatever you decide to tell Harry Phelps or the state police, you have no proof. Nothing. Maybe people would start whispering behind my back and pointing out Billy as the man who killed Rowdy Beddoe but that would be all. Billy wouldn't go to prison or stand trial or even be arrested and neither would I."

"Chances are you're right, Sheriff. But then there's always that chance, slim as it may be, that some piece of evidence will pop up that will reveal the truth."

Claxton's eyes narrow in anger.

"You're a real hard case, aren't you, Joe?"

"I try not to be," I say.

"I'm giving you every chance to walk away from here and you don't want to take any of them."

"Like I said before, I'm stupid that way."

I watch as his hand clasps the grip of his revolver.

"You're not going to shoot me, Sheriff. You can't explain me away. Besides, abetting Billy Boggs in the accidental death of someone like Rowdy Beddoe is one thing. Cold blooded murder is something else and you haven't got it in you."

His eyes never leave mine and then I see his hand relax and

move away from his gun.

At that moment, we hear a man's voice call out.

"Sheriff Claxton!"

We turn to look as two Texas Highway Patrol officers come around the edge of the billboard.

"Here you are," one of them says. "We've been looking all over for you for the past hour. Lucky we spotted your car." He looks from Claxton to me and back to Claxton. "Everything okay here?" he asks curiously.

"Yes, fine," Claxton says. "No problem."

"Good. We need you to come with us, Sheriff. One of your deputies showed up this morning at headquarters in Alpine to make a statement about the death of Rowdy Beddoe and we need you to come with us and clarify a few things."

Claxton nods.

"All right.," he says. He looks over at me. "The keys to the cruiser are in the ignition, Joe. Drive it back to the station, will you, please?"

"Sure," I say.

Claxton nods with a wry half smile on his lips and then he turns and starts to walk back to the road with the two Highway Patrolmen right behind him.

EPILOGUE

Weeks have passed. Marfa is a memory. Principal photography has been completed. The editing process has begun and George Stevens has barricaded himself in an editing room, cutting and splicing and rearranging, all the little things that spell the difference between a bad movie and a good one or a good one and a great one. Stevens may be meticulous but his resume is rife with great motion pictures so even Jack Warner leaves him alone. The cascade of publicity that spewed forth while the film was shooting has slowed to a small but steady trickle. At some point I will be told a release date and then I will again swing into action, starting slowly and building to world-blanketing coverage a few days before the premiere. I have seen a lot of footage. This is going to be a terrific movie. Rock Hudson, often underrated as an actor, has never been better. James Dean,whom I was sure had been miscast, is a wonder to watch. He has colors I didn't know existed.

Billy Boggs no longer works as a deputy for the Presidio County Sheriff's Department. Sam Claxton is no longer the Sheriff. With the approval of J.W. Beddoe, neither man was indicted for his part in the death of Rowdy Beddoe or the subsequent coverup. Billy moved out of state. No one knows where he went. Sam Claxton was given a chance to retire with a pension and he accepted. I'm told he is running a small private security firm in the area and is doing well. The false front Reata ranch house is still standing and won't be dismantled. The town fathers have high hopes that it will become a tourist attraction. They may be right. I am between major commitments and have started another novel. This one's about a happy-go-lucky bachelor in his thirties who gets himself suckered into siring a daughter by a woman who wants the daughter but wants no part of him. Hmm. Wonder where that idea came from. In fairness to Jill, she has come around generously and while I am still kindly 'Uncle Joe", I get access to Yvette whenever I want.

For instance, now.

I am sitting on a blanket on Malibu Beach doodling with the day's crossword puzzle. Yvette, now a lively two-and-a-half-year old chatterbox, is sitting a few feet away with a pail and shovel constructing something which I believe is supposed to be a castle but looks more like a lopsided stack of pancakes. Every minute or two, on cue, I tell her how terrific it is. She giggles and goes about making improvements. Jill is in an office in downtown L.A. conferring with her publishing company's lawyer who is suing the crap out of a rival publisher for plagiarism. Eight months ago Jill came up with a dancing piglet in a tutu called Pretty Prancing Peggy. Sales of that book have been in the tens of thousands. Suddenly there appears on the scene a dancing groundhog in a kilt named Tippy Toe Thomas. Blood will run in the streets before this is over if I know my Jill.

"Okay, kiddo, time to go," I say as I check my watch. It's creeping up on five o'clock and on this 30th day of September, darkness is setting in earlier and earlier.

"Awww, Unca Joe," she whines. "Just five more minutes." This is her favorite phrase. She learned it a few months ago and now she cannot live without it. It seems particularly useful at bedtime and when watching old cartoons on television.

"Don't you remember, Yvette, we just did five minutes five minutes ago, didn't we?"

"I don't remember," she says guilelessly.

"Besides the ice cream man is going to close up any minute now so we have to hurry."

She is now galvanized into action, putting on her little terry cloth robe and scooping up her pail, shovel, water wings and flippers. I get to my feet and sling our blanket and towels over my shoulder as we head for the parking area next to Rte. 1. The ice cream wagon is still there and Yvette opts for a vanilla cone. The man has his portable radio on and I only get a piece of the broadcast as I pay him and we walk away.

"......eyewitnesses say the white sports car was forced to swerve to avoid a head on collision and was hit hard enough to send it flying through the air about twenty yards from the intersection. California Highway Patrol, says that traffic is now backed up on Rt. 46 for at least two miles and motorists are advised to avoid this route if at all possible. Neither of the drivers of the cars involved have been identified at this time...."

On the way home, I flip on a top 40 music station and Yvette squeals with delight when Little Richard comes on the air singing 'Tutti Fruitti'. Her favorite song. She's also partial to anything by Bill Haley and the Comets.

I drop her off at the front door into the loving arms of Jill's housekeeper Bridget O'Shaughnessy. Jill's not back yet from the lawyers. I tell Bridget I'll call later. Back in my car I head for the Valley and my modest little house in Van Nuys. I'm singing along with Tennessee Ernie Ford about some number nine coal when the song is suddenly interrupted for a news bulletin.

"James Dean is dead."

I stare at the radio is disbelief.

"A spokesman for the California Highway Patrol has confirmed that Dean was killed in an automobile accident on State Route 46 approximately two hours ago. A passenger in Dean's car, identified as Rolph Weutherich, is in serious condition at Paso Robles

Hospital with a broken leg and head injuries. Dean, a rising star in Hollywood, came to fame in the films, 'Rebel Without a Cause' and 'East of Eden' and the recently completed film 'Giant'. Dean was 24 years old at the time of his death...."

The reporter drones on. I half hear him. This is a tragedy. A young man so full of life and a life so full of promise, snuffed out in an instant. No doubt at some time in the next day or two, some priest or minister will tell us it was God's will. If that is so it's no wonder I have so little use for God.

When I get home I turn on the television set. The story is now being reported on every channel. I turn up the volume so I can hear while I brew a pot of coffee in the kitchen. By now there is more information. Dean was on his way to Salinas to compete in a road race driving his newly purchased car, a Porsche 550 Spyder. The accident came about when Dean tried unsuccessfully to swerve to avoid a collision with a Ford being driven by a man named Donald Turnupseed. Turnupseed escaped with a minor gash on his head. Tomorrow morning I will be at work early. My phone will be ringing constantly as newspapers and magazines dig for stories about this charismatic young man whose life was cut short far too soon. I will give them all something to write about, even if I have to invent it. The screenwriter James Warner Bellah once told me he was doodling with a theme for a movie about an iconic figure who had died leaving behind a larger-than-life reputation that might not really be deserved. His theme? When the legend becomes fact, print the legend. I have this feeling deep inside that James Dean will not soon be forgotten and the legend will endure.

The End

AUTHOR'S NOTE

I have no doubt that Marfa, Texas, is a delightful place in which to grow up. Has been and always will be and because of 'Giant' it will always have a place in film history. So please forgive me if you feel that Marfa has in any way been maligned in this story. It was not my intention. All of the Marfa natives are fictional starting with the Sheriff and his deputies as well as the tortured Dr. Yardley and the young clinic doctor, Roger Troy. J.W. Beddoe and his son are also figments of my imagination and if there was such a family in and around Marfa at the time of the filming, I am unaware of it. The only actual people depicted herein are the stars and other professionals involved in the making of the motion picture. These people have my deep respect and nothing written here should be interpreted as an attempt to disparage or demean. As predicted it took George Stevens over a year to edit the film to his satisfaction but in the end his meticulous care paid off. 'Giant' was lavishly praised by the critics and much loved by the public. It was the highest grossing film ever released by Warner Brothers until 'Superman' in 1978. It received 10 Academy Award nominations including Best Actor (both Hudson and Dean), Best Supporting Actress (McCambridge), Best Picture and Best Screenplay. The only winner was George Stevens who was honored as Best Director. James Dean appeared in only three motion pictures but his legacy continues to grow year after year and today his name can be found listed among the best actors to ever appear on the screen. Let it be noted here that among Dean's favorite pastimes in Marfa was going out into the desert in the dead of night with a .22 rifle and a lamp on his head to shoot jackrabbits. That is not legend, that is fact. I found many sources to be helpful in portraying the background of this movie location accurately but one in particular was extremely helpful, 'Going Hollywood', by Kirby F. Warnock. It's a fun read and you can find it when you click on 'James Dean' on your computer.

ABOUT THE AUTHOR

Peter S. Fischer is a former television writer-producer who currently lives with his wife Lucille in the Monterey Bay area of Central California. He is a co-creator of "Murder, She Wrote" for which he wrote over 40 scripts. Among his other credits are a dozen "Columbo" episodes and a season helming "Ellery Queen." He has also written and produced several TV mini-series and Movies of the Week. In 1985 he was awarded an Edgar by the Mystery Writers of America. In addition to four EMMY nominations, two Golden Globe Awards for Best TV series, and an Anthony Award from the Boucheron, he has received the IBPA award for the Best Mystery Novel of the Year, a Bronze Medal from the Independent Publishers Association and an Honorable Mention from the San Francisco Festival for his first novel.

Available at Amazon.com

www.petersfischer.com

PRAISE FOR THE HOLLYWOOD MURDER MYSTERIES

Jezebel in Blue Satin

n this stylish homage to the detective novels of Hollywood's Golden Age, a ress agent stumbles across a starlet's dead body and into the seamy world of cheming players and morally bankrupt movie moguls.....An enjoyable fast-aced whodunit from opening act to final curtain.

—Kirkus Reviews

ans of golden era Hollywood, snappy patter and Raymond Chandler will nd much to like in Peter Fischer's murder mystery series, all centered on ld school studio flak, Joe Bernardi, a happy-go-lucky war veteran who nds himself immersed in tough situations.....The series fills a niche that's en superseded by explosions and violence in too much of popular culture ld even though jt's a world where men are men and women are dames, its impses at an era where the facade of glamour and sophistication hid an glier truth are still fun to revisit.

—2012 San Francisco Book Festival, Honorable Mention

zebel in Blue Satin, set in 1947, finds movie studio publicist Joe Bernardi mming it at a third rate motion picture house running on large egos and tle talent. When the ingenue from the film referenced in the title winds up ad, can Joe uncover the killer before he loses his own life? Fischer makes an ortless transition from TV mystery to page turner, breathing new life into e film noir hard boiled detective tropes. Although not a professional sleuth, e's evolution from everyman into amateur private eye makes sense; any bad blicity can cost him his job so he has to get to the bottom of things.

—ForeWord Review

We Don't Need No Stinking Badges

A thrilling mystery packed with Hollywood glamour, intrigue and murder, set in 1948 Mexico.....Although the story features many famous faces (Humphrey Bogart, director John Huston, actor Walter Huston and novelist B. Traven, to name a few), the plot smartly focuses on those behind the scenes. The big names aren't used as gimmicks—they're merely planets for the story to rotate around. Joe Bernardi is the star of the show and this fictional tale in a real life setting (the actual set of 'Treasure of the Sierra Madre' was also fraught with problems) works well in Fischer's sure hands....A smart clever Mexican mystery.

—Kirkus Reviews

A former TV writer continues his old-time Hollywood mystery series, seamlessly interweaving fact and fiction in this drama that goes beyond the genre's cliches. "We Don't Need No Stinking Badges" again transports reader to post WWII Tinseltown inhabited by cinema publicist Joe Bernardi... Strong characterization propels this book. Toward the end the crosses and double-crosses become confusing, as seemingly inconsequential things such as a dead woman who was only mentioned in passing in the beginning now become matters on which the whole plot turns (but) such minor hiccups should not deter mystery lovers, Hollywood buffs or anyone who adores a good yarn.

—ForeWord Review

Peter S. Fischer has done it again—he has put me in a time machine and landed me in 1948. He has written a fast paced murder mystery that will have you up into the wee hours reading. If you love old movies, then this is the book for you.

—My Shelf. Com

This is a complex, well-crafted whodunit all on its own. There's plenty of action and adventure woven around the mystery and the characters are fully fashioned. The addition of the period piece of the 1940's filmmaking and the inclusion of big name stars as supporting characters is the whipped cream and cherry on top. It all comes together to make an engaging and fun read.

—Nyssa, Amazon Customer Review

Love Has Nothing to Do With It

Fischer's experience shows in 'Love Has Nothing To Do With It', an homage to film noir and the hard-boiled detective novel. The story is complicated... but Fischer never loses the thread. The story is intricate enough to be intriguing but not baffling....Joe Bernardi's swagger is authentic and entertaining. Overall he is a likable sleuth with the dogged determination to uncover the truth.... While the outcome of the murder is an unknown until the final pages of the current title, we do know that Joe Bernardi will survive at least until 1950, when further adventures await him in the forthcoming 'Everybody Wants an Oscar'.

–Clarion Review

A stylized, suspenseful Hollywood whodunit set in 1949....Goes down smooth for murder-mystery fans and Old Hollywood junkies.

–Kirkus Review

The Hollywood Murder Mysteries just might make a great Hallmark series. Let's give this book: The envelope please: FIVE GOLDEN OSCARS.

–Samfreene, Amazon Customer Review

The writing is fantastic and, for me, the topic was a true escape into our past entertainment world. Expect it to be quite different from today's! But that's why readers will enjoy visiting Hollywood as it was in the past. A marvelous concept that hopefully will continue up into the 60s and beyond. Loved it!

–GABixlerReviews

The Unkindness of Strangers

*Winner of the Benjamin Franklin Award
for Best Mystery Book of 2012
by the Independent Book Publisher's Association.*

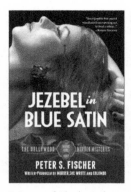

Book One—1947
JEZEBEL IN BLUE SATIN

WWII is over and Joe Bernardi has just returned home after three years as a war correspondent in Europe. Married in the heat of passion three weeks before he shipped out, he has come home to find his wife Lydia a complete stranger. It's not long before Lydia is off to Reno for a quickie divorce which Joe won't accept. Meanwhile he's been hired as a publicist by third rate movie studio, Continental Pictures. One night he enters a darkened sound stage only to discover the dead body of ambitious, would-be actress Maggie Baumann. When the police investigate, they immediately zero in on Joe as the perp. Short on evidence they attempt to frame him and almost succeed. Who really killed Maggie? Was it the over-the-hill actress trying for a comeback? Or the talentless director with delusions of grandeur? Or maybe it was the hapless leading man whose career is headed nowhere now that the "real stars" are coming back from the war. There is no shortage of suspects as the story speeds along to its exciting and unexpected conclusion.

Book Two—1948
WE DON'T NEED NO STINKING BADGES

Joe Bernardi is the new guy in Warner Brothers' Press Department so it's no surprise when Joe is given the unenviable task of flying to Tampico, Mexico, to bail Humphrey Bogart out of jail without the world learning about it. When he arrives he discovers that Bogie isn't the problem. So-called accidents are occurring daily on the set, slowing down the filming of "The Treasure of the Sierra Madre" and putting tempers on edge. Everyone knows who's behind the sabotage. It's the local Jefe who has a finger in every illegal pie. But suddenly the intrigue widens and the murder of one of the actors throws the company into turmoil. Day by day, Joe finds himself drawn into a dangerous web of deceit, dupliciity and blackmail that nearly costs him his life.

Book Three—1949
LOVE HAS NOTHING TO DO WITH IT

Joe Bernardi's ex-wife Lydia is in big, big trouble. On a Sunday evening around midnight she is seen running from the plush offices of her one- time lover, Tyler Banks. She disappears into the night leaving Banks behind, dead on the carpet with a bullet in his head. Convinced that she is innocent, Joe enlists the help of his pal, lawyer Ray Giordano, and bail bondsman Mick Clausen, to prove Lydia's innocence, even as his assignment to publicize Jimmy Cagney's comeback movie for Warner's threatens to take up all of his time. Who really pulled the trigger that night? Was it the millionaire whose influence reached into City Hall? Or the not so grieving widow finally freed from a loveless marriage. Maybe it was the partner who wanted the business all to himself as well as the new widow. And what about the mysterious envelope, the one that disappeared and everyone claims never existed? Is it the key to the killer's identity and what is the secret that has been kept hidden for the past forty years?

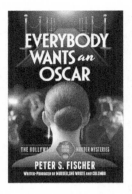

Book Four—1950
EVERYBODY WANTS AN OSCAR

After six long years Joe Bernardi's novel is at last finished and has been shipped to a publisher. But even as he awaits news, fingers crossed for luck, things are heating up at the studio. Soon production will begin on Tennessee Williams' "The Glass Menagerie" and Jane Wyman has her sights set on a second consecutive Academy Award. Jack Warner has just signed Gertrude Lawrence for the pivotal role of Amanda and is positive that the Oscar will go to Gertie. And meanwhile Eleanor Parker, who has gotten rave reviews for a prison picture called "Caged" is sure that 1950 is her year to take home the trophy. Faced with three very talented ladies all vying for his best efforts, Joe is resigned to performing a monumental juggling act. Thank God he has nothing else to worry about or at least that was the case until his agent informed him that a screenplay is floating around Hollywood that is a dead ringer for his newly completed novel. Will the ladies be forced to take a back seat as Joe goes after the thief that has stolen his work, his good name and six years of his life?

Book Five—1951
THE UNKINDNESS OF STRANGERS

Warner Brothers is getting it from all sides and Joe Bernardi seems to be everybody's favorite target. "A Streetcar Named Desire" is unproducible, they say. Too violent, too seedy, too sexy, too controversial and what's worse, it's being directed by that well-known pinko, Elia Kazan. To make matters worse, the country's number one hate monger, newspaper columnist Bryce Tremayne, is coming after Kazan with a vengeance and nothing Joe can do or say will stop him. A vicious expose column is set to run in every Hearst paper in the nation on the upcoming Sunday but a funny thing happens Friday night. Tremayne is found in a compromising condition behind the wheel of his car, a bullet hole between his eyes. Come Sunday and the scurrilous attack on Kazan does not appear. Rumors fly. Kazan is suspected but he's not the only one with a motive. Consider:

Elvira Tremayne, the unloved widow. Did Tremayne slug her one time too many?

Hubbell Cox, the flunky whose homosexuality made him a target of derision.

Willie Babbitt, the muscle. He does what he's told and what he's told to do is often unpleasant.

Jenny Coughlin, Tremayne's private secretary. But how private and what was her secret agenda?

Jed Tompkins, Elvira's father, a rich Texas cattle baron who had only contempt for his son-in-law.

Boyd Larabee, the bookkeeper, hired by Tompkins to win Cox's confidence and report back anything he's learned.

Annie Petrakis, studio makeup artist. Tremayne destroyed her lover. Has she returned the favor?

Book Six—1952
NICE GUYS FINISH DEAD

Ned Sharkey is a fugitive from mob revenge. For six years he's been successfully hiding out in the Los Angeles area while a $100, 000 contract for his demise hangs over his head. But when Warner Brothers begins filming "The Winning Team", the story of Grover Cleveland Alexander, Ned can't resist showing up at the ballpark to reunite with his old pals from the Chicago Cubs of the early 40's who have cameo roles in the film. Big mistake. When Joe Bernardi, Warner Brothers publicity guy, inadvertently sends a press release and a photo of Ned to the Chicago papers, mysterious people from the Windy City suddenly appear and a day later at break of dawn, Ned's body is found sprawled atop the pitcher's mound. It appears that someone is a hundred thousand dollars richer. Or maybe not. Who is the 22 year old kid posing as a 50 year old former hockey star? And what about Gordo Gagliano, a mountain of a man, who is out to find Ned no matter who he has to hurt to succeed? And why did baggy pants comic Fats McCoy jump Ned and try to kill him in the pool parlor? It sure wasn't about money. Joe , riddled with guilt because the photo he sent to the newspapers may have led to Ned's death, finds himself embroiled in a dangerous game of who-dun-it that leads from L. A. 's Wrigley Field to an upscale sports bar in Altadena to the posh mansions of Pasadena and finally to the swank clubhouse of Santa Anita racetrack.

Book Seven—1953
PRAY FOR US SINNERS

Joe finds himself in Quebec but it's no vacation. Alfred Hitchcock is shooting a suspenseful thriller called "I Confess" and Montgomery Clift is playing a priest accused of murder. A marriage made in heaven? Hardly. They have been at loggerheads since Day One and to make matters worse their feud is spilling out into the newspapers. When vivacious Jeanne d'Arcy, the director of the Quebec Film Commisssion volunteers to help calm the troubled waters, Joe thinks his troubles are over but that was before Jeanne got into a violent spat with a former lover and suddenly found herself under arrest on a charge of first degree murder. Guilty or not guilty? Half the clues say she did it, the other half say she is being brilliantly framed. But by who? Fingers point to the crooked Gonsalvo brothers who have ties to the Buffalo mafia family and when Joe gets too close to the truth, someone tries to shut him up. . . permanently. With the Archbishop threatening to shut down the production in the wake of the scandal, Joe finds himself torn between two loyalties.

Book Eight–1954
HAS ANYBODY HERE SEEN WYCKHAM?

Everything was going smoothly on the set of "The High and the Mighty" until the cast and crew returned from lunch. With one exception. Wiley Wyckham, the bit player sitting in seat 24A on the airliner mockup, is among the missing, and without Wyckham sitting in place, director William Wellman cannot continue filming. A studio wide search is instituted. No Wyckham. A lookalike is hired that night, filming resumes the next day and still no Wyckham. Except that by this time, it's been discovered that Wyckham, a British actor, isn't really Wyckham at all but an imposter who may very well be an agent for the Russian government, The local police call in the FBI. The FBI calls in British counterintelligence. A manhunt for the missing actor ensues and Joe Bernardi, the picture's publicist, is right in the middle of the intrigue. Everyone's upset, especially John Wayne who is furious to learn that a possible Commie spy has been working in a picture he's producing and starring in. And then they find him . It's the dead of night on the Warner Brothers backlot and Wyckham is discovered hanging by his feet from a streetlamp, his body bloodied and tortured and very much dead. and pinned to his shirt is a piece of paper with the inscription "Sic Semper Proditor". (Thus to all traitors). Who was this man who had been posing as an obscure British actor? How did he smuggle himself into the country and what has he been up to? Has he been blackmailing an important higher-up in the film business and did the victim suddenly turn on him? Is the MI6 agent from London really who he says he is and what about the reporter from the London Daily Mail who seems to know all the right questions to ask as well all the right answers.

Book Nine—1955
EYEWITNESS TO MURDER

Go to New York? Not on your life. It's a lousy idea for a movie. A two year old black and white television drama? It hasn't got a prayer. This is the age of CinemaScope and VistaVision and stereophonic sound and yes, even 3-D. Burt Lancaster and Harold Hecht must be out of their minds to think they can make a hit movie out of "Marty". But then Joe Bernardi gets word that the love of his life, Bunny Lesher, is in New York and in trouble and so Joe changes his mind. He flies east to talk with the movie company and also to find Bunny and dig her out of whatever jam she's in. He finds that "Marty" is doing just fine but Bunny's jam is a lot bigger than he bargained for. She's being held by the police as an eyewitness to a brutal murder of a close friend in a lower Manhattan police station. Only a jammed pistol saved Bunny from being the killer's second victim and now she's in mortal danger because she knows what the man looks like and he's dead set on shutting her up. Permanently. Crooked lawyers, sleazy con artists and scheming businessmen cross Joe's path, determined to keep him from the truth and when the trail leads to the sports car racing circuit at Lime Rock in Connecticut, it's Joe who becomes the killer's prime target.

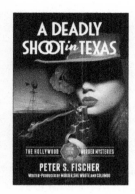

Book Ten—1956
A DEADLY SHOOT IN TEXAS

Joe Bernardi's in Marfa, Texas, and he's not happy. The tarantulas are big enough to carry off the cattle , the wind's strong enough to blow Marfa into New Mexico, and the temperature would make the Congo seem chilly. A few miles out of town Warner Brothers is shooting Edna Ferber's "Giant" with a cast that includes Rock Hudson, Elizabeth Taylor and James Dean and Jack Warner is paying through the nose for Joe's expertise as a publicist. After two days in Marfa Joe finds himself in a lonely cantina around midnight, tossing back a few cold ones, and being seduced by a gorgeous student young enough to be his daughter. The flirtation goes nowhere but the next morning little Miss Coed is found dead . And there's a problem. The coroner says she died between eight and nine o'clock. Not so fast, says Joe, who saw her alive as late as one a.m. When he points this out to the County Sheriff, all hell breaks loose and Joe becomes the target of some pretty ornery people. Like the Coroner and the Sheriff as well as the most powerful rancher in the county, his arrogant no-good son and his two flunkies, a crooked lawyer and a grieving father looking for justice or revenge, either one will do. Will Joe expose the murderer before the murderer turns Joe into Texas road kill? Tune in.

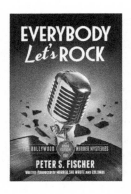

Book Eleven—1957
EVERYBODY LET'S ROCK

Big trouble is threatening the career of one of the country's hottest new teen idols and Joe Bernardi has been tapped to get to the bottom of it. Call it blackmail or call it extortion, a young woman claims that a nineteen year old Elvis Presley impregnated her and then helped arrange an abortion. There's a letter and a photo to back up her claim. Nonsense, says Colonel Tom Parker, Elvis's manager and mentor. It's a damned lie. Joe is not so sure but Parker is adamant. The accusation is a totally bogus and somebody's got to prove it. But no police can be involved and no lawyers. Just a whiff of scandal and the young man's future will be destroyed, even though he's in the midst of filming a movie that could turn him into a bona fide film star. Joe heads off to Memphis under the guise of promoting Elvis's new film and finds himself mired in a web of deceit and danger. Trusted by no one he searches in vain for the woman behind the letter, crossing paths with Sam Philips of Sun Records, a vindictive alcoholic newspaper reporter, a disgraced doctor with a seedy past, and a desperate con artist determined to keep Joe from learning the truth.

Book Twelve–1958
A TOUCH OF HOMICIDE

It takes a lot to impress Joe Bernardi. He likes his job and the people he deals with but nobody is really special. Nobody, that is, except for Orson Welles, and when Avery Sterling, a bottom feeding excuse for a producer, asks Joe's help in saving Welles from an industry-wide smear campaign, Joe jumps in, heedless that the pool he has just plunged into is as dry as a vermouthless martini. A couple of days later, Sterling is found dead in his office and the police immediately zero in on two suspects—Joe who has an alibi and Welles who does not. Not to worry, there are plenty of clues at the crime scene including a blood stained monogrammed handkerchief, a rejected screenplay, a pair of black-rimmed reading glasses, a distinctive gold earring and petals from a white carnation. What's more, no less than four people threatened to kill him in front of witnesses. A case so simple a two-year old could solve it but the cop on the case is a dimwit whose uncle is on the staff of the police commissioner. Will Joe and Orson solve the case before one of them gets arrested for murder? Will an out-of-town hitman kill one or both of them? Worst of all, will Orson leave town leaving Joe holding the proverbial bag?

Available in paperback or Kindle editions from Amazon.com

Made in the USA
Las Vegas, NV
05 March 2023

68590468R00125